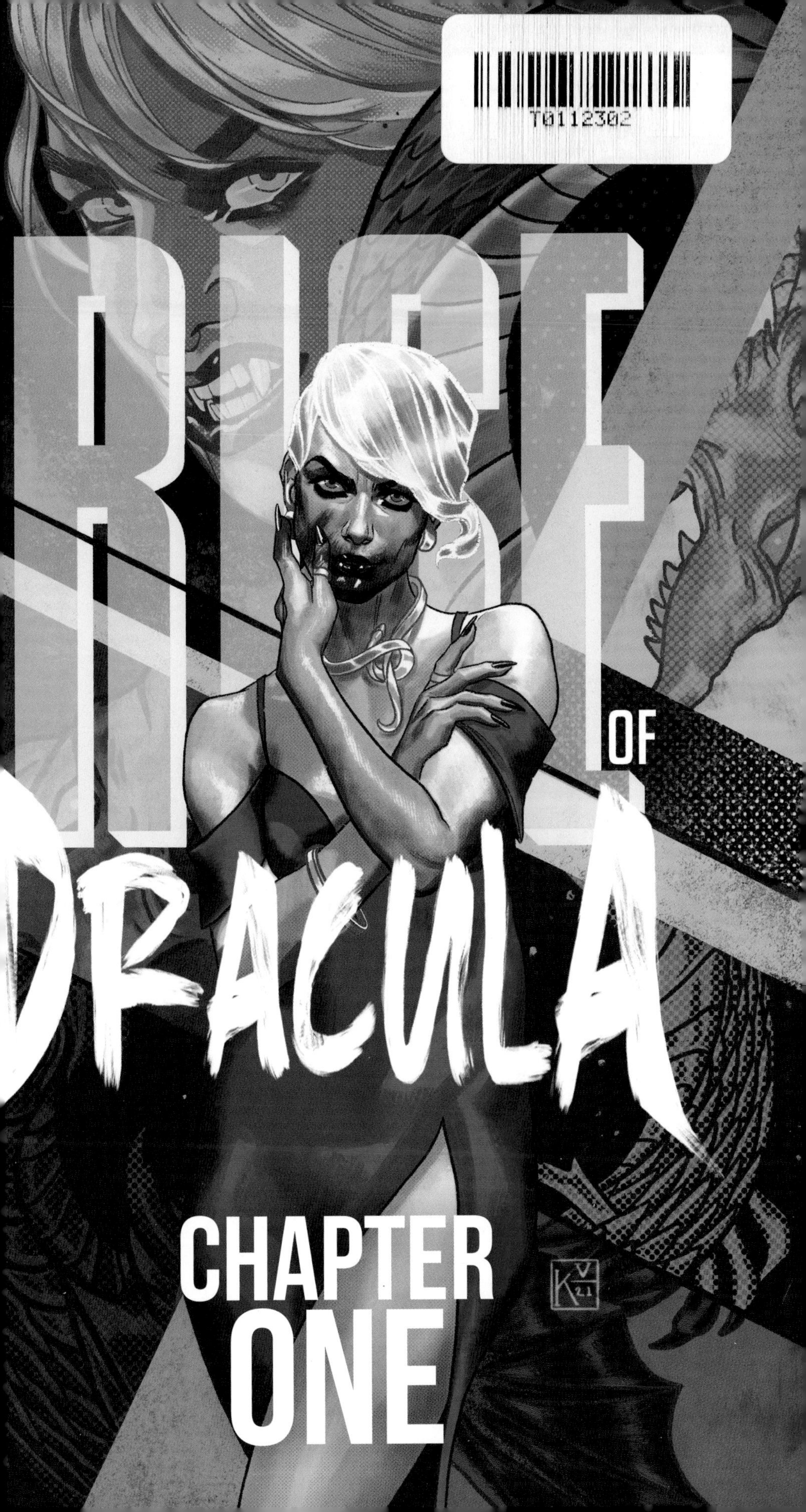
RISE
OF
DRACULA
CHAPTER
ONE

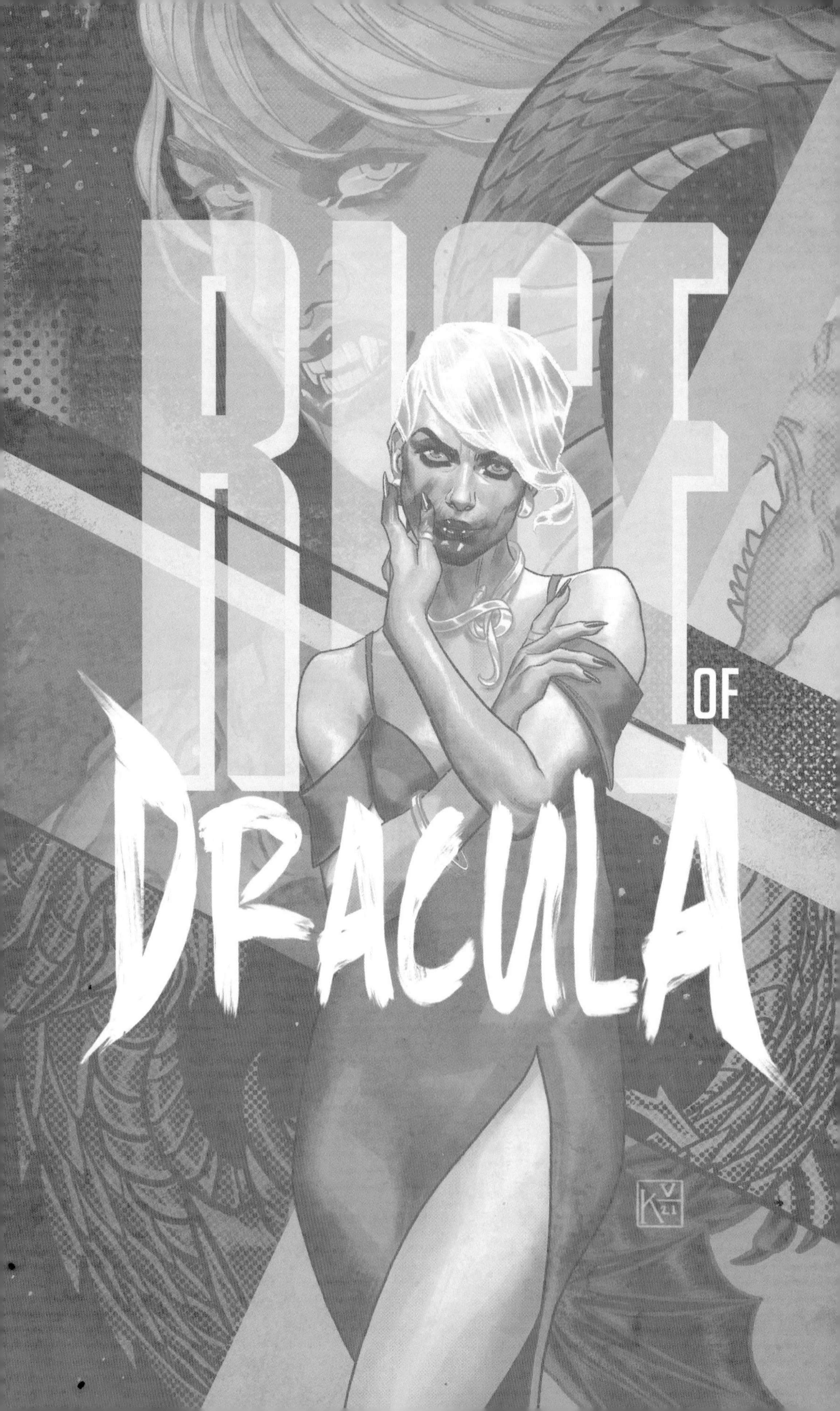
RISE
OF
DRACULA

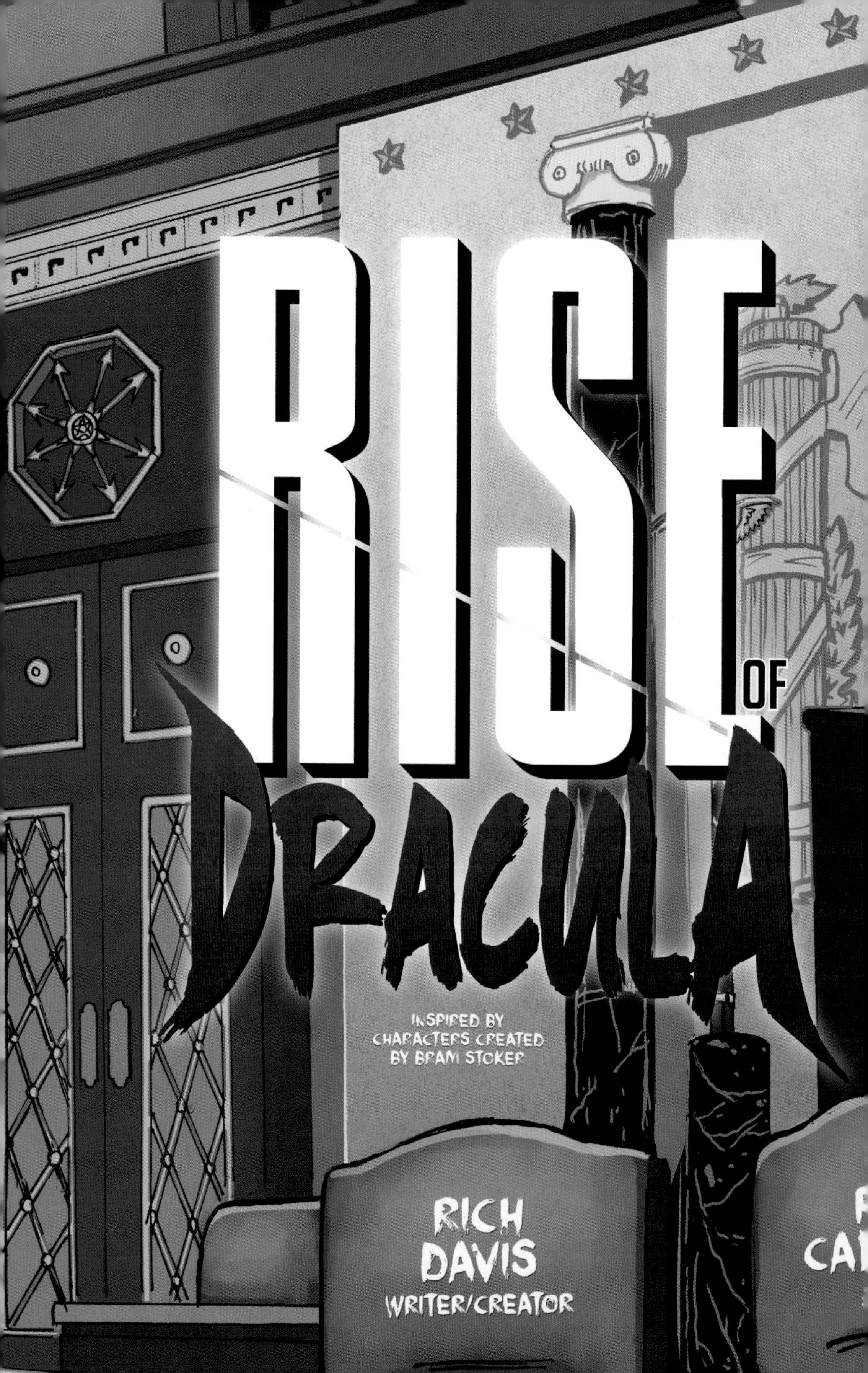
RISE OF DRACULA
INSPIRED BY CHARACTERS CREATED BY BRAM STOKER
RICH DAVIS
WRITER/CREATOR

I WARNED THEM. THEY WOULDN'T LISTEN.
THEY NEVER DO.
ALEX ZIEF
COLORS
DAVE LENTZ
LETTERS/DESIGN
PAUL PITTINGER
EXECUTIVE PRODUCER
AMBER DAVIS
EDITOR

VRRRMMM

RUN!!
BLAM
SPLUT
WAAHHHHH
WAAHHHHHHHH
AAAIEEEEEEEEEEEE

Reagan International Airport
HUFF
HUFF
RRRUMM
BLE
VRRR
M

THE INVASION IS GOING EXCEPTIONALLY WELL, MINISTER.
OUR INFILTRATION SQUADS SUCCESSFULLY ENCITED VIOLENCE AT OUR PROTEST RALLIES...
LIBERATION. WE'RE CALLING IT A LIBERATION. IT GOES DOWN EASIER.
AS YOU SAY, MINISTER.
.. AND WE'RE PEACEKEEPERS, NOT INFILTRATORS. THEY'RE RIOTS, NOT PROTESTS.
THIS IS A PROACTIVE RESPONSE TO PROTECT THE PEOPLE FROM DOMESTIC TERRORISTS AND THUGS WHO INTEND TO DESTROY OUR WAY OF LIFE...
"OUR PROCESSING CENTERS ARE FUNCTIONING EFFICIENTLY. WE'LL HAVE THE CAMPS FULLY STOCKED... "
"FARMS. THEY'RE FARMS NOW.... DIDN'T YOU READ THE MEMO?"
APOLOGIES, MINISTER. I MUST HAVE MISSED IT.
MAKE SURE EVERYONE CHECKS THE EMAILS FOR CHANGES. PROPAGANDA IS A PRECISE SCIENCE.
WE DRIVE THE NARRATIVE BY USING THE CORRECT VERBIAGE.

DO NOT WORRY, MOTHERS, WE HAVE STAFF TO TAKE CARE OF YOUR CHILDREN. ALL WILL BE AS IT SHOULD.
JACK GRIFFIN, MD
GENETICS
PLEASE PROCEED TO YOUR DESIGNATED QUE. YOU'LL FIND THEY ARE ARRANGED BY AGE.
ALL IS WELL.

STOP HER!
KRAK
WUMP
KRUNCH
ANYONE ELSE?
NO? GOOD.
NO MORE DISTURBANCES.
EXECUTE TWELVE MORE AT RANDOM.
IF THEY CANNOT LOVE US, THEY *WILL* FEAR US.

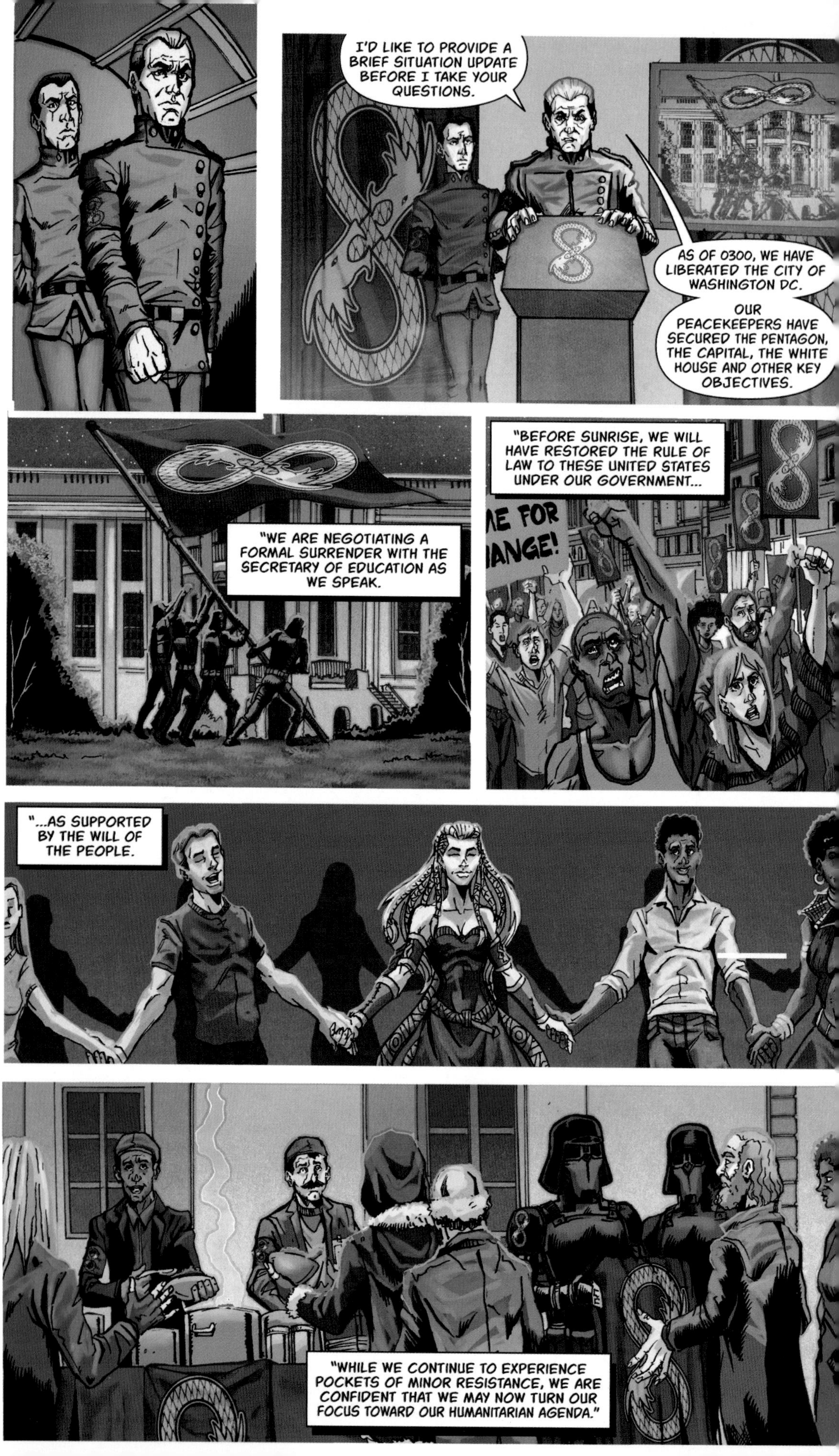
I'D LIKE TO PROVIDE A BRIEF SITUATION UPDATE BEFORE I TAKE YOUR QUESTIONS.
AS OF 0300, WE HAVE LIBERATED THE CITY OF WASHINGTON DC.
OUR PEACEKEEPERS HAVE SECURED THE PENTAGON, THE CAPITAL, THE WHITE HOUSE AND OTHER KEY OBJECTIVES.
"WE ARE NEGOTIATING A FORMAL SURRENDER WITH THE SECRETARY OF EDUCATION AS WE SPEAK.
"BEFORE SUNRISE, WE WILL HAVE RESTORED THE RULE OF LAW TO THESE UNITED STATES UNDER OUR GOVERNMENT...
"...AS SUPPORTED BY THE WILL OF THE PEOPLE.
"WHILE WE CONTINUE TO EXPERIENCE POCKETS OF MINOR RESISTANCE, WE ARE CONFIDENT THAT WE MAY NOW TURN OUR FOCUS TOWARD OUR HUMANITARIAN AGENDA."

YOU'RE LATE.
PATROLS EVERYWHERE. SLOWED US DOWN.
FUCK THAT!
YOU PICKED UP STRAYS. THAT SLOWED YOU DOWN.
...ANNDDD YOU WERE FOLLOWED. PERFECT!
OME OUT.
T DOWN.
PRETEND I'M ABOUT TO RIP YOUR THROAT OUT.
OH! YOU'VE GOT THAT PART ON LOCK. GOOD JOB!

MMPH
MMMMM, MMM, MMNH! WHAT IS IT ABOUT THE END OF THE WORLD THAT MAKES PEOPLE SO GODDAMN HORNY?
IT'S LIKE, 'OH MY GOD! IT'S A VAMPIRE APOCALYPSE. LET'S FUCK!'
HEH HEH...
...WAIT...IT'S THE END OF THE WORLD?
NOT FOR US, DUMBASS. FOR THEM!

OH SHIT! DRACULINA...WE... WE THOUGHT...
WE DIDN'T...
...FUCK!
TRAUTMAN! LET'S LEAVE DRACULINA TO HER... PRIVACY.
WAIT...
...WHY ARE THERE KIDS HERE?
GODDAMMIT.
NGHH
WHY DID YOU HAVE TO LOOK BACK?
THOK

JESUS!
THIS IS ALL YOUR FAULT!
I DIDN'T WANT TO DO THIS!
SCHRIP
LUCY...CALM DOWN...
SKRAK
DON'T TELL ME TO CALM DOWN!
WHAK
I TOLD YOU TO STAY AWAY FROM DC!
I TOLD YOU TO COME ALONE!
I TOLD YOU!
DID YOU LISTEN?
NO! OF COURSE NOT! YOU. NEVER. FUCKING. LISTEN!
I GOT YOU A JEEP. TAKE IT. YOU AND YOUR STRAYS GET OUT OF DC.
DON'T COME BACK.
I CAN'T HELP YOU ANYMORE.

ARTHUR...
BE CAREFUL...

WOOOOOOOOOOOO!!!
HA HA HA HA HA
YEAH!
OH SHIT!
SKREEEEEEE
UNGH!
WHUMP

HHSSSSS!
AAAIEEEEEEEEEEE
Y'ALL GO ON!
I'LL CATCH UP.
WE NEED TO TALK ABOUT IMPULSE CONTROL.
SHE'S GOING TO RUIN HER DINNER.
SHE'S GOING TO GET FAT!
OH MY GOD, YESSSSS!
FEAR!
I LOVE THAT SMELL!
STOMP
YEAHHHH!
U-STREET
DISTRICT

The Bronze
THE WORLD IS OURS!
CALM DOWN THERE, SCARFACE.
WE'VE JUST TAKEN DC. WE'LL TAKE THE WORLD TOMORROW!
BUT FIRST, WE GET FUCKED UP!
IT'S AMAZING HOW MANY FUCKBOIS MISS THE ENTIRE POINT OF SCARFACE.
NEVER GET HIGH ON YOUR OWN SUPPLY!
APROPOS...
LET'S BE HYPOCRITES!
YAAAAASSSSSS
GOODBYE CRUEL WORLD!
REMEMBER 'COOL WORLD'?
I SAID CRUEL WORLD...BUT YES, I DO.
I HAD SUCH A CRUSH ON THAT CHICK.
HOLLI WOULD IF SHE COULD. SO HOT!
SO FUCKING HOT!

EEP BEEP BEEP
FRESH MEAT!
HUH?
BURP
SHIT, ELLIE! AGAIN?!
THEY'RE GOING TO BE PISSED!
A GIRL'S GOTTA EAT!

RELAX, BILLY!
THEY WON'T DO ANYTHING TO ME.
NO, BUT THEY MIGHT MURDER ME. LITERALLY.
TECHNICALLY IT WOULDN'T BE "MURDER." MURDER IS AN UNLAWFUL KILLING.
THEY'RE WELL WITHIN THEIR RIGHTS TO EXECUTE YOU FOR FUCKING UP ON DUTY.
GO TO HELL, ELLIE!
YOU AND YOUR LAW DEGREE.
BILLY...
NO. JUST NO.
BUT...I WANT IT...
I NEED IT.
THIS IS THE LAST TIME...

GODDAMMIT!

O
BABS
RUTHVEN
LARA
RUTHVEN

ELLIE RUTHVEN
VAUGHN

HEY! WHAT ARE YOU--
SPLORT
EEEEW! GROSS!
GIVE 'EM HELL, BOYS!

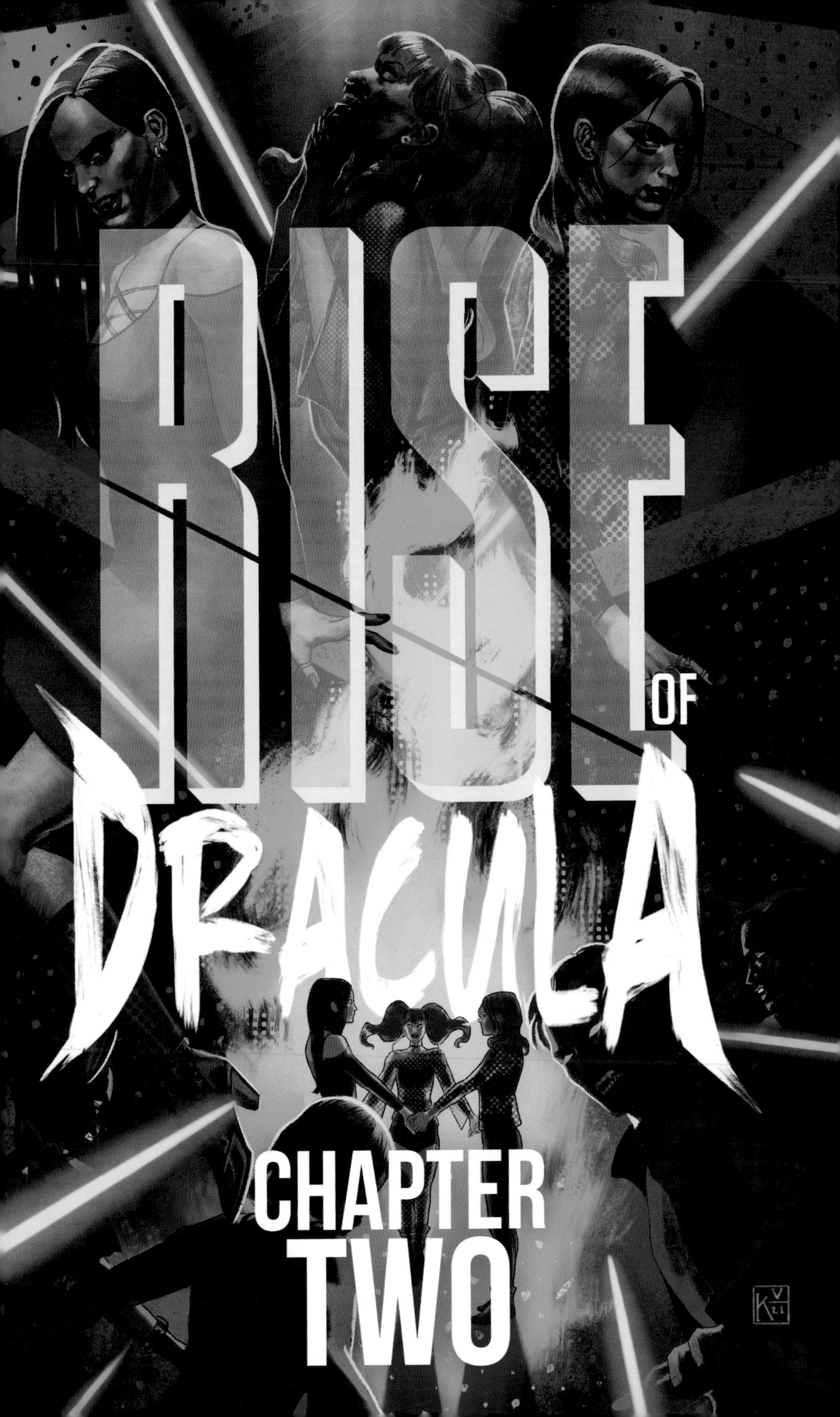
RISE
OF
DRACULA
CHAPTER
TWO

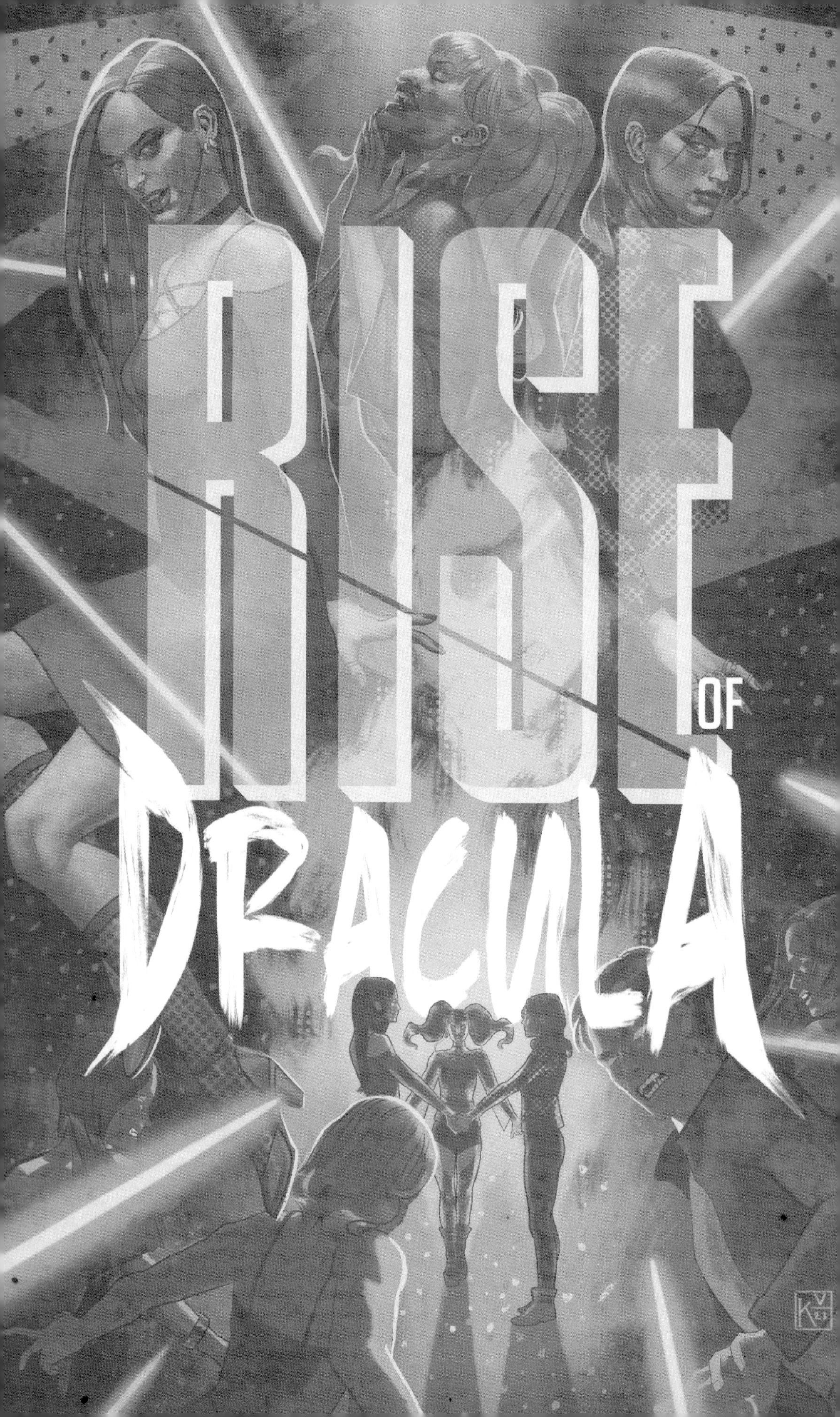
RISE
OF
DRACULA

BLAM
BLAM
SKREEEEE!!
BLAM
BLAM
BLAM
BLAM
FOOMP
BLAM
BLAM
BLAM
WHOOSH

CARMILLA! WE HAVE A SITUATION.
SHOW ME.
TEMPLAR KNIGHTS ARE ASSAULTING A RAVE ON U-STREET.
TAP
WE HAVE URBAN ASSAULT DRONES, YES?
WE DO.
USE THEM.
WE'LL HIT OUR OWN PEOPLE.
YES, BUT WE'LL HIT THEIRS AS WELL.

YOU GONNA COME OVER AND TALK OR JUST STARE AT ME LIKE A CREEPER?
HOW'D YOU KNOW?
I'M A FUCKING VAMPIRE PRINCESS. I HEARD YOU COMING FROM THE ARTS OF PEACE.
A NINJA YOU ARE NOT, SIR.
YOU KNOW I DANCED BALLET FOR YEARS. I AUDITIONED FOR JULLIARD.
DID YOU GET IN?
NO.
WELL THEN...

WHY ARE YOU HERE, ARTHUR?
I TOLD YOU TO STAY OUT OF DC.
I KNOW.
WHEN SHE CATCHES YOU, I CAN'T HELP YOU.
I KNOW.
I WON'T...
I KNOW.
THEN WHY ARE YOU HERE?
I NEED YOUR HELP.
I KNOW.
FUCK! WHAT DO YOU NEED?

WE'RE HITTING A SHIPMENT. KIDS. ON THEIR WAY TO THE FARMS.
WE'RE GETTING THEM AWAY FROM YOUR PSYCHO SISTER.
SHE'S NOT PSYCHOTIC.
SHE COMMITTED GENOCIDE.
HER METHODS SUCK...BUT SHE'S NOT WRONG.
HOW CAN YOU SAY THAT?
DO YOU HEAR SIRENS?
NO.
GUNSHOTS?
...

HOW MANY HOMELESS PEOPLE DID YOU PASS ON YOUR WAY HERE?
THE AIR IS CLEAN. SO IS THE WATER. NO ONE IS STARVING.
POVERTY. DOESN'T. EXIST.
BUT...
NO! NO BUTS. YOUR KIND FAILED.
MY KIND?
OH FUCK OFF! HUMANS! YOU KNEW WHAT I MEANT.
YOU CALL IT GENOCIDE. SHE CALLS IT MERCY. IT'S ALL PERSPECTIVE AND POINT OF VIEW.
HOW CAN MURDERING SEVEN HUNDRED THOUSAND INNOCENT PEOPLE BE MERCIFUL?
STOP BEING SO DRAMATIC!
IT WAS LESS THAN FIVE HUNDRED THOUSAND. AND THEY WEREN'T INNOCENT.
THE REST ARE IN CAMPS JUST WAITING TO BE MURDERED.
NOT ALL OF THEM.
WE NEED BREEDERS. WE WANT PETS.

BREEDERS? PETS? CAN YOU HEAR YOURSELF RIGHT NOW?
HUMANS HAD TWO HUNDRED THOUSAND YEARS.
WHAT DID YOU DO WITH ALL THAT TIME?
YOU FOUGHT WARS. YOU RAPED. YOU MURDERED. YOU DROVE 99.9% OF EVERY THING THAT EVER LIVED INTO EXTINCTION.
YOU SUCKED THE PLANET DRY OF EVERY POSSIBLE RESOURCE.
YOU WERE GIVEN PARADISE AND YOU MADE IT YOUR TOILET.
I DON'T FEEL SORRY FOR YOU. WHY SHOULD I? YOU'RE A SPECIES OF PERPETUAL TODDLERS.
YOU'VE PROVEN YOU CAN'T BE LEFT ALONE.
YOU NEED CONSTANT SUPERVISION.
I'M SORRY YOU'RE HAVING TROUBLE ADJUSTING TO A NEW APEX PREDATOR, BUT YOU SHOWED US WHAT TO DO.
WE'RE JUST BETTER AT IT.
WILL YOU HELP ME?
...YES...

SHE'LL DO IT.

BLAM
BLAM
HA HA HA HA HA HA HA
I AM WAY TOO FUCKING HIGH FOR THIS!
ELLIE!
ON YOUR FEET, BITCH!

BELET-SERI, WE BESEECH YOU, OPEN YOUR BOOKS OF THE DEAD.
IZANAMI-NO-MIKOTO, WE BESEECH YOU, INVITE SOULS TO QUICKEN THESE CORPSES.
DEA TACITA, WE BESEECH YOU, TURN THEM TOWARD THOSE WHO MEAN US HARM.
HINE-NUI-TE-PŌ, WE BESEECH YOU, PAINT THE WORLD RED WITH THEIR BLOOD!
GREAT MOTHERS PROTECT US. WE BESEECH YOU!
SPLUT
SPLUT
BLAM
SCHUK

BLAM
BLAM
BLAM
AAAIEEEEEEEEEEE
PSST PSST
BRAKKA
BRAKKA
BRAKKA
BRAKKA
BRAKKA
SPLUT
SPLUT
SPLUT
CLANG
SCHLICK
BOGGIN BAWBAG!

DRACULINA.
YIP YIP
I NEED TO SEE MY SISTER.
I'M AFRAID THAT'S NOT POSSIBLE, DRACULINA.
WHY?
IT'S ALRIGHT, DOLORES. SEND HER IN.
OF COURSE, DRACULA.
MY APOLOGIES, DRACULINA. I WAS MISTAKEN.
THANK YOU, DOLORES.

LUCY!
SMEK
GENTLEMEN, I NEED A MOMENT WITH MY SISTER.
THIS WAY. WE'LL RECONVENE IN THE CABINET ROOM.
ONLY A MOMENT. YOU STILL HAVE THE FIVE FAMILIES AND YOUR NIGHTLY WAR BRIEFING ON THE AGENDA.
LADY RUTHVEN WANTS FIVE MINUTES BEFORE THE STATE DINNER...
THANK YOU, CARMILLA. THAT WILL BE ALL.
DRACULA.

I'M SO HAPPY YOU'RE HERE. I CAN JUST BE MINA. FUCK DRACULA.
I THOUGHT YOU WANTED THIS?
I DID. I DO. IT'S STILL A BURDEN.
EVERYONE HATES ME.
NO... MINA...
THE U.N. LABELED ME A WAR CRIMINA
I'VE BEEN EXCOMMUNICATED
CONDEMNED A
TAKFIR AND THEY DECLARED CHERE
AGAINST ME.
SOMEHOW I'VE BECOME THE DEVIL AFTER I SENT THE LITERAL DEVIL STRAIGHT TO HELL.
WHY CAN'T THEY SEE? I'M ONLY SAVING THEM FROM THEMSELVES!
I'M SORRY.
YOU WANTED TO TALK AND HERE I AM RAMBLING ON ABOUT THINGS YOU DON'T UNDERSTAND.

YOU NEVER NEED TO APOLOGIZE OR EXPLAIN YOURSELF TO ME. EVER.
YOU'RE MY SISTER. I LOVE YOU. I ALWAYS WILL. COME WHAT MAY.
THANK YOU.
NOW, WHAT IS IT YOU WANTED TO TALK ABOUT?
THE FARMS...
WE'VE BEEN OVER THIS, LULU. THE FARMS ARE...
TERRIBLE?
...NECESSARY.
YOU CAN'T POSSIBLY BELIEVE THAT.
I ABSOLUTELY DO.
HOW? WE WERE DOING FINE WITHOUT THEM. WITHOUT ALL OF THIS.
BUT THEY WEREN'T.

THEIR WORLD WAS DYING. THEY WERE KILLING IT.
I KNOW... BUT...
NO BUTS. HUMANITY IS A PLAGUE. WE CAN NO LONGER ALLOW IT TO GO UNTREATED.
LUCY, I GET IT. I CAN BARELY LOOK AT MYSELF IN THE MIRROR...
SPEAKING OF, WERE YOU AS SURPRISED AS I WAS WHEN YOU FOUND OUT WE STILL HAD REFLECTIONS?
HAHAHA YES!
I WAS SERIOUSLY WORRIED! HOW WAS I GOING TO TAKE OVER THE WORLD IF I COULDN'T EVEN DO MY OWN MAKEUP?
MAKEUP? REALLY? THAT'S WHAT YOU WERE WORRIED ABOUT WHILE YOU WERE PLANNING GENOCIDE?
NO...KIND OF... WE ALL HAVE OUR BAUBLES OF VANITY--
KABOOOM

WHAT WAS THAT?
I DON'T KNOW.
APOLOGIES, DRACULA.
YOU'RE NEEDED IN THE SITUATION ROOM.
I HAVE TO GO NOW. I HAVE WORK.
MINA...YOU'RE IN DANGER...
HAHAHAHAHAHAHA
I'M ALWAYS IN DANGER. THE ENTIRE PLANET WANTS ME DEAD.
NO! IMMEDIATE DANGER.
THE RESISTANCE PLANNING TO ATTACK THE FARMS. IT'S A TRAP.
CLEARLY.
I THINK HEY INTEND TO SSASSINATE YOU.
AND YOU KNOW THIS HOW?
...
ARTHUR.
...

YOU STILL LOVE HIM?
...I DO...

BRAKKA
BRAKKA
BRAKKA
RRRGGHHH!
SPLUT
TSSS
TSSS
TSSS
TSSS
WHUP WHUP WHUP
KRASH

THIS JUST IN. YOU'RE LOOKING AT A DISTURBING LIVE SHOT OF THE WAREHOUSE DISTRICT NEAR U STREET IN WASHINGTON, DC.
THE TRANSITION OF POWER IN THE UNITED STATES APPEARS LESS PEACEFUL THAN THE NEW ORDO DRACUL GOVERNMENT HAS LED US TO BELIEVE...
ARE DEMOCRATS SNEAKING NANO-SPY-BOTS INTO YOUR DRINKING WATER? FOX NEWS REPORTS. YOU DECIDE. NEXT.
WHITE HOUSE SOURCES TELL US THAT A GROUP CALLING THEMSELVES THE NEW SOLDIERS OF SOLOMON HAVE CLAIMED CREDIT FOR THIS BRUTAL ACT OF TERRORISM.

White House
CASUALTIES ARE WAY BEYOND PROJECTIONS.
AND THE RUTHVEN GIRLS!?
WHAT THE FUCK HAPPENED ABE? WHY WERE THEY THERE?
I DON'T KNOW.
LADY RUTHVEN IS BLAMING DRACULA. IT'S ALL OVER TWITTER.
I'LL HANDLE IT.
YOU'D BETTER!
WE NEED HER INFLUENCE. THIS ALL FALLS APART WITHOUT HER.
I AM MORE THAN AWARE.
HOW DO WE SPIN IT?
TERRORISTS. THUGS. DEVIANTS. SAME WAY WE HANDLE ANY ACTIVIST UPRISING. WE MAKE HER DAUGHTERS INTO MARTYRS.
THAT MIGHT WORK FOR BABS AND LARA. BUT...
ELLIE.
I HAVEN'T SEEN A MONSTER LIKE HER IN 400 YEARS.
SHE'S WHAT YOU'D GET IF THE JOKER AND HARLEY QUINN DID BATH SALTS AND MADE A METH ADDICTED, SCHIZOPHRENIC BABY.
THAT'S ELLIE.
THANK YOU ALL FOR COMING.

DAMASKINOS, RUTHVEN, ORLOCK, MANDURUGO, DRACULA. EACH OF THE GREAT HOUSES IS SEATED AT THIS TABLE. WE ARE ***NOT*** EQUAL, YET WE ARE UNITED.
OUR STORIES PREDATE THE ACKNOWLEDGMENT OF TIME. OUR SOULS WEAR THE SCARS OF MANY PLOTS, DECEPTIONS AND BETRAYALS.
WE HAVE FORGOTTEN MOST OF THE REASONS WE HAVE TO DISTRUST EAC OTHER. NONE OF THAT MATTERS.

WE CANNOT MOVE FORWARD WHILE LOOKING BACK. NO REPARATION TODAY WILL REPAIR THE DAMAGE DONE CENTURIES AGO. WE LIVE TOGETHER OR WE PERISH ALONE.
WE ARE THE PEACEMAKERS. OUR WAY IS TRUTH. TRUTH IS LIFE. LIFE IS SACRIFICE.
TAKE THEM THIS MESSAGE. ***MAKE*** THEM SEE. THERE IS MORE TO LIFE THAN CONSUMPTION.
GREED AND GLUTTONY STARVE US ALL. MAKE THEM SEE. WE ARE THEIR ONLY HOPE. MAKE THEM SEE!

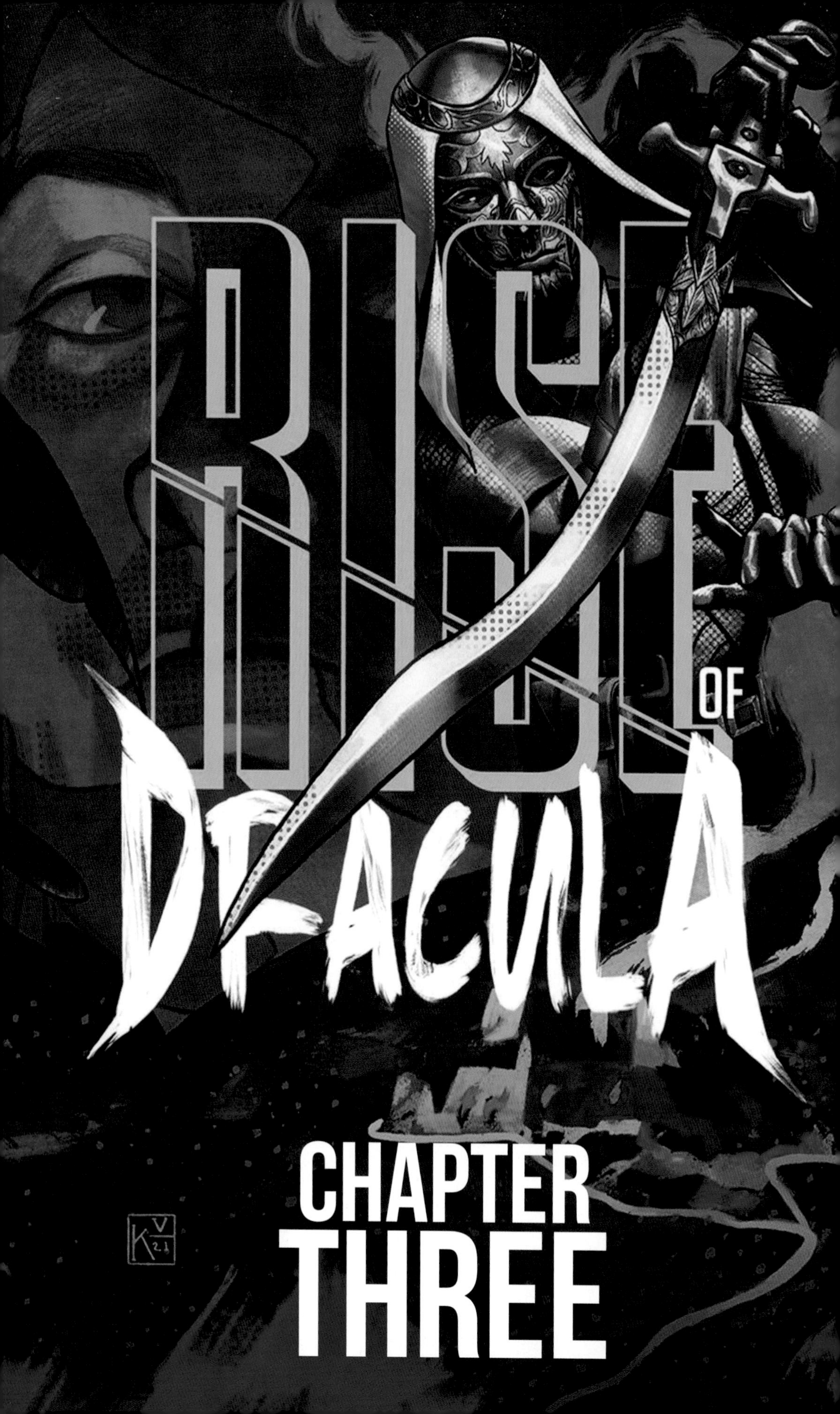
RISE OF
DRACULA
CHAPTER
THREE

esistance Campsite.
SARGE?
WHAT IS IT BOY?
GRRRRR
GRRRRR

I MAY NOT LIVE TO SEE OUR GLORY.
BUT I WILL GLADLY JOIN THE FIGHT.
AND WHEN OUR CHILDREN TELL OUR STORY--
THEY'LL TELL THE STORY OF TONIGHT...
I LOVE HAMILTON. I WISH WE COULD HAVE SEEN IT ON BROADWAY.
SOMEDAY. WHEN THIS IS ALL OVER

BORK
BORK
BORK
BORK
JESUS GODDAMN CHRIST!
BORK
BORK
HA HA HA HA HA

BLAM
NO, NOT TONIGHT.

YOU CAN DANCE!
YOU CAN JIVE!
HAV-ING. THE TIME OF YOUR LIIIFE!
OOOOO-OOO!
BOTTLE SERVICE!
YAAAASSSS QUEEN!
DO YOU EVER THINK THIS IS EXCESSIVE?
EVEN FOR US?
IT'S ABSOLUTELY EXCESSIVE!
YOU ONLY GO TO HELL ONCE, RIGHT?

SHUT THE FUCK UP, SYLVIA!
SYLVIA?
PLATH? SHE STUCK HER HEAD IN AN OVEN.
YOUR HEAD'S IN A JAR.
SHE WROTE THE BELL JAR...
YOU KNOW WHAT? IF I HAVE TO EXPLAIN IT, IT'S NOT FUNNY ANYMORE.
BETTER TO RULE IN HELL THAN SERVE IN HEAVEN.
GODS-DAMNED RIGHT!
SIGH
WHAT? ARE WE SUPPOSED TO MOPE AROUND ALL SAD AND PENITENT?
FUCK THAT!
FUCK THAT!
OK, BUT SERIOUSLY, WE'VE GOTTA DO SOMETHING. WE'RE MORE THAN COMIC RELIEF... RIGHT?
LOOK AT YOU GETTING ALL EXISTENTIALLY META!
PLIP
SIGH

HA HA HA HA HA HA HA HA HA HA HA HA HA HA HA HA HA HA
I MEAN, WHAT'S THE POINT?
IT'S NOT LIKE WE'RE EVER GETTING OUT OF HERE.
MIGHT AS WELL ENJOY IT!
ALL THE FUN, DECADENT STUFF IS HERE ANYWAY.
UMMM, GUYS...
...WHERE IS MY BODY?
UMMM...
YOU BOTH GOT YOURS BACK... WHY AM I JUST A BAD FUTURAMA REFERENCE?
I LOVE THAT SHOW. EXCEPT THE DOG EPISODE.
CAN'T WATCH THAT ONE. TOO SAD!
ELLIE! I'M SERIOUS! WHERE'S MY FUCKING BODY?
BITCH, I DON'T KNOW! I GOT HERE THE SAME TIME AS YOU.

IT'S OK, BABSY-BOO. I'M SURE IT'LL TURN UP.
IT'S A BODY WITH NO HEAD.
IF IT DIDN'T GET BLOWN UP...
...SOMEONE'S PROBABLY USING IT FOR A COMMUNITY THEATRE PRODUCTION OF SLEEPY HOLLOW OR SOMETHING.
YOU THINK SOMEONE HAS IT!?
NOOOO...
PROBABLY.
I WONDER WHAT HE'S DOING WITH IT RIGHT NOW?
WHO?
THE NORMAN BATES WEIRDO WHO HAS YOUR BODY.
I'M GOING TO BE SICK!
HOW?
YOU AIN'T GOT NO GUTS LT. DAN!
FUCK YOU ELLIE!

Baghras Castle, Turkey
HAYYA ALAS SALAH!
HAYYA ALAS SALAH!
HNN
HAYYA ALAL FALAH!
HYA!!
HAYYA ALAL FALAH!
HRRM.

SCREEEEEEEE
SCREEEEE
SCREE
SUBJECT 01271945. ORGAN REGENERATION IS CONSISTENT WITH PREVIOUS EXPERIMENTS.

AAAIIEEE
PROGRESS, VICTOR?
MINIMAL AT BEST.
WE NEED THIS TO WORK.
THEN LEAVE ME TO DO MY WORK, TALUS.

AKASHA HAS TAKEN NORTH AFRICA FOR THE ORDO DRACUL, GRAND MASTER. CAIRO WAS OUR LAST HOLDOUT.
PARLIAMENT VOTED TO JOIN THE MOVEMENT TODAY.
WE'RE SEEING A RISE IN PRO-DRACULA SENTIMENT ACROSS THE EU AS WELL.
SIGNE HAS A TALENT FOR ROUSING THE RABBLE.
BALLOU
LANDRY
...AND ASIA?
NO WORD, GRAND MASTER.
IT'S BEEN RADIO SILENCE SINCE THE CCP MET WITH AKUMU SIX WEEKS AGO.
THANK YOU, BROTHERS. YOU ARE DISMISSED.
GRAND MASTER.
I PRAY YOU BRING ME GOOD TIDINGS, BROTHER TALUS.
I DO NOT, GRAND MASTER.
PROBLEM WITH YOUR SOLDIERS?
NO, GRAND MASTER. MY **PROBLEM** IS WITH THE WAR!
OR, PERHAPS I SHOULD SAY, THE LACK THEREOF.

WE ARE A WELL TRAINED, WELL ARMED AND HIGHLY MOTIVATED ORDER. WE ARE READY TO FIGHT, BUT THERE IS NO WAR TO BE FOUGHT!
THE WORLD IS GIVING IN TO DRACULA WITHOUT A *FIGHT!*
UTOPIA IS AN APPEALING MESSAGE.
WHY WOULD DESPERATE PEOPLE RESIST PROMISES OF FULL BELLIES, WARM SHELTERS AND THE END OF DISEASE?
THE GREAT BEAST OF THE EARTH WAS GIVEN AUTHORITY OVER EVERY NATION.
ALL INHABITANTS OF THE EARTH WILL TAKE ITS MARK AND WORSHIP IT.

BROTHER VICTOR?
HE'S A FRUSTRATING, ARROGANT SON OF A BITCH. BUT, HE'S BLOODY BRILLIANT.
IF ANY MAN CAN UNLOCK THE MYSTERIES OF THE UNDEAD, IT'S HIM.
I DON'T LIKE TO BE SPIED UPON. IT SUGGESTS A LACK OF TRUST.
TRUST IS EARNED, BROTHER.
DOCTOR. IT'S DOCTOR.
"I CAN ALREADY REANIMATE THE DEAD...
"...BUT I JUST CAN'T STOP THEM FROM EATING EVERYTHING IN SIGHT."
DRACULA WAS RIGHT. HUMANS ARE FUNDAMENTALLY FLAWED!
THANK YOU, BROTHER.
FUCK OFF!

KITTY-CAT ON A SECURE CHANNEL, GRAND MASTER.
PUT IT THROUGH.
AYE, SIR.
NACHASH IS ALONE. NOW IS THE TIME.
DANKE.
AYE, GRAND MASTER.
DĀBBAT AL-ARD!
DĀBBAT AL-ARD. REPEAT. DĀBBAT AL-ARD. ALL TEAMS. DĀBBAT AL-ARD.

VRRRMM
DRACULA! YOU CAME BACK!
OF COURSE I DID!
I PROMISED YOU I WOULD.
SITUATION REPORT?
PAPA GOT THE MILKERS WORKING TODAY. PAPA SAYS WE CAN RUN THREE SHIFTS NOW.

PAPA SAYS THAT'S A THOUSAND GALLONS EVERY SINGLE DAY.
PAPA SAYS WE COULD GET MORE IF HE HAD MORE **GOD-DAMNED** STOCK!
IS THAT SO?
OOOPS!
I WASN'T S'POSED TO SAY THAT LAST PART.
IT'S OKAY, MOLLY.
I'M SORRY, MA'AM.
SHE RAN OFF AS SOON AS SHE HEARD YOU COMING.

SHE'S NO BOTHER.
JONATHAN. ARTHUR. THIS IS ISAIAH.
HE'S THE OVERSEER OF THIS FARM, BUT MOLLY IS THE REAL BOSS 'ROUND THESE PARTS."
A PLEASURE.
MY FRIENDS NEED A SAFE PLACE TO STAY. WE HAVE ROOM RIGHT?
WE CAN'T IMPOSE...
PLENTY!
STAY AS LONG AS YOU'D NEED. LEAVE WHENEVER YOU'D LIKE. YOU'RE NOT PRISONERS HERE. NO ONE IS.
THIS ISN'T WHAT I EXPECTED.
WHAT DID YOU EXPECT?
I DON'T KNOW. SOMETHING MORE SCHINDLER'S LIST?
I'M A VAMPIRE, JONATHAN. I'M NOT A MONSTER.
I WON'T LIE TO YOU, JONATHAN. THIS IS A FARM. ONE OF MANY. THINGS HAPPEN HERE.
NECESSARY THINGS...BUT THINGS THAT YOU MAY FIND TROUBLING.

YOU GREW UP ON A FARM. YOU KNOW THIS IS WHERE FOOD COMES FROM.
OH GOD!
HWARGGH
BU--BU-- BUT...THEY'RE PEOPLE...
WHY DOES THAT MATTER?
ONE BILLION CHILDREN... JUST LIKE MOLLY...ARE **STARVING.**
RIGHT NOW. IN YOUR WORLD.
ONE. BILLION. YOU CAN'T PROVIDE FOR THE PEOPLE YOU HAVE, YET YOU JUST KEEP BREEDING!
THIS IS A MERCY.
SPLUT
WELL... SHIT...

SCREEEEE SCREE
SCREEE
AAAIIEEE
HSSSS
HSSSS
NOOOOOOOOOOOOO!
WHAT THE?
I WILL FIND YOU AGAIN.
NOOOOOOOOOOOOOOOO!
DRACULA IS DEAD.
LONG LIVE DRACULA.

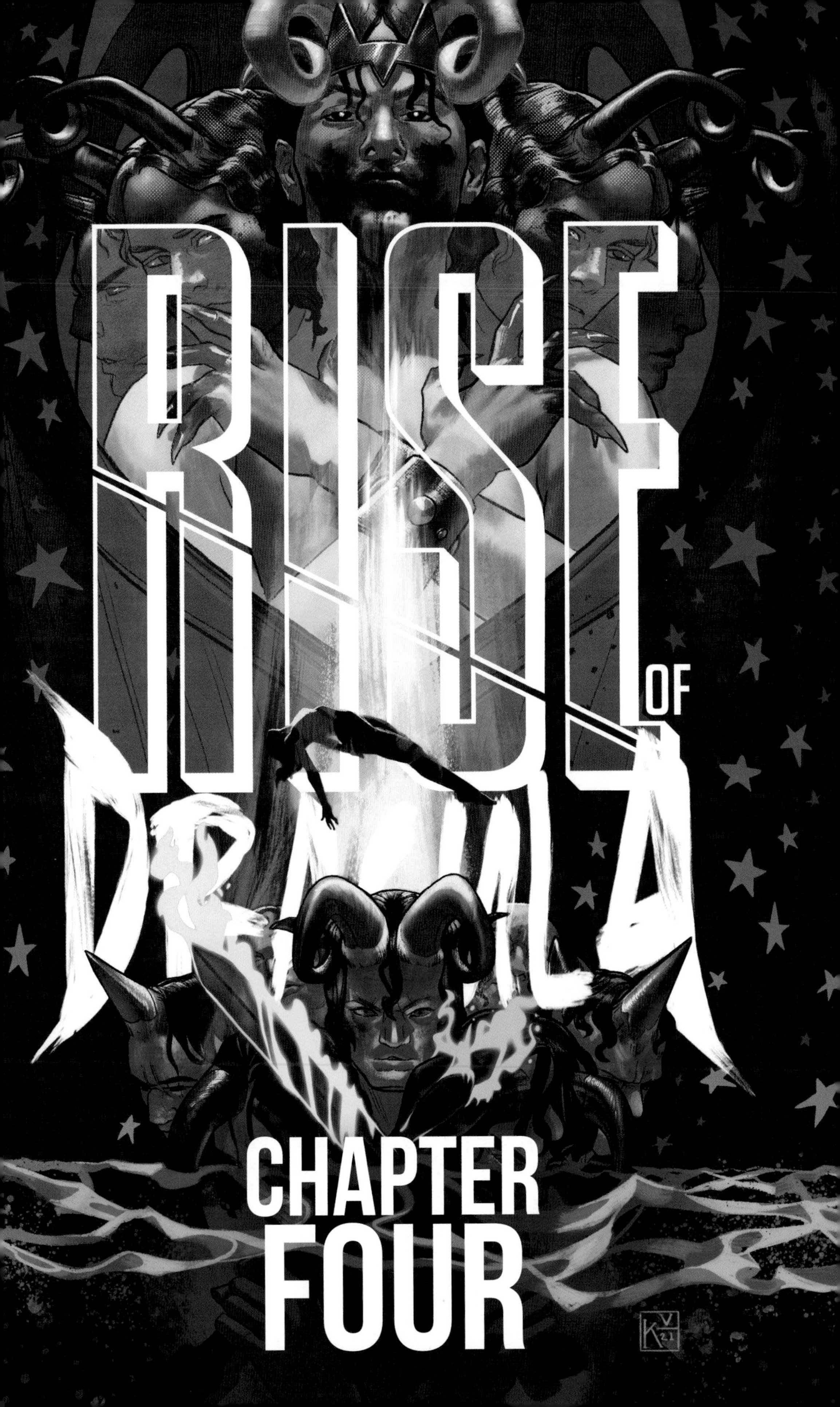
RISE OF
CHAPTER FOUR

RISE OF

S Capitol
BA-DUM
BA-DUM
BA-DA-DA-DA-
DA-DA-DUM
BA-DUM
BA-DUM
BA-DA-DA-DA-
DA-DA-DUM

WE'RE BRINGING YOU LIVE COVERAGE OF DRACULA'S FUNERAL...
DRACULA'S FUNERAL 19:
abc NEWS
COFFEE BEAN
FFEE EAN
COFFEE BEAN
CIT
...BORN WILHELMINA PATRICK MURRAY, THE CONTROVERSIAL REFORMER WAS ASSASSINATED WHILE LEADING A GOODWILL TOUR OF THE HILLINGHAM AGRICULTURAL COLLECTIVE.
•LIVE
HILLINGHAM IS ONE OF TEN RE-EDUCATION COMMUNES ESTABLISHED BY THE ORDO DRACUL TO HOUSE REFUGEES DISPLACED BY AMERICA'S WAR ON MARGINALIZED COMMUNITIES...
DRACULA'S MESSAGE REJECTING IDENTITY POLITICS RESONAT WITH FREEDOM FIGHTERS EVERYWHERE.
•LIVE
THE MOVEMENT IS FORCING OPPRESSOR NATIONS AROUND THE WORLD TO IMPLEMENT IMMEDIATE REFORMS...
CBS NEWS DRACULA'S MOURNERS 19:05
BBC NEWS
IN A TIME OF UNPARALLELED DIVISION, THE SOCIAL CRUSADER TURNED REVOLUTIONARY STUNNED THE WORL BY LEADING A BLOODLESS COUP THAT TOPPLED THE AMERICAN GOVERNMENT...
•LIVE
DRACULA HAS FINALLY DELIVERED A CHANGE WE CAN BELIEVE IN.
Bloomberg NEWS

I CAN'T DO THIS.
YOU CAN, LOVE. I PROMISE.
WHEN I BECAME DRACULA...
I'M NOTHING LIKE YOU! YOU WERE BORN TO DO THIS. YOU WERE GROOMED TO BE DRACULA.
I WASN'T EVEN SUPPOSED TO HAPPEN! I SHOULDN'T BE HERE!
BUT YOU ARE HERE.
YOU DO EXIST AND YOU WILL DO THIS. YOU MUST.
IT'S NOT FAIR!
SHE'S RIGHT, MOTHER, IT ISN'T FAIR.
YOU'VE ALWAYS BEEN HER CHAMPION. YOUR LOVE FOR YOUR SISTER IS COMMENDABLE, BUT FOOLISH.
THE ABOMINATION SHOULD HAVE BEEN DROWNED THE MOMENT IT WAS BORN.
THERE CAN BE ONLY ONE DRACULA IN ANY AGE. SO IT IS WRITTEN.
WELL, NOW THERE IS.
BECAUSE I'M...YOU KNOW... DEAD.

YOU CAN'T FUCK YOUR WAY THROUGH THIS ONE.
YOU WERE NEVER WANTED.
YOU. ARE. NOTHING.
THEY WILL NEVER ACCEPT YOU.
YOU'RE A PRETTY FACE. NOTHING MORE
THIS WAS NOT MEANT FOR YOU.

YOU WILL FAIL.
THEY SEE RIGHT THROUGH YOU.
THEY WILL REJECT YOU.
I NEVER WANTED THIS! I DON'T WANT IT. I DON'T...

WHO ARE YOU SPEAKING TO, DRACULA?
CARMILLA!
UMMM... NO ONE... I WAS JUST TALKING TO MYSELF.
PARDON ME, DRACULA, BUT IT'S TIME.
DO I HAVE TO DO THIS? I'M NOT READY. YOU DO IT. I...
JUST READ THE SPEECH THAT ABRAHAM HAS PREPARED.
OUR PRESS OFFICE WILL TAKE IT FROM THERE.
WE'VE ALREADY MADE ARRANGEMENTS WITH SOCIAL MEDIA COMPANIES TO ENSURE OUR MESSAGE GETS ACROSS AS WE INTEND IT.
FINE.

AUOV UAD AUON ACNUROP IAS IICINECU ERTAC IULUNMOD ASIZ...AIUTSECA IULUSACAL IULUTNAFS IA IROTACAFENIB IS IROTIULIM IROTANIHCNI.
UEZENMUD IUL ROLIBOR ROLETACAP AERATREI IS AERASAL AERATE-CREC AERIUTNAM AETATANAS AECAP ATAIV...
...ALIM URTNEP MAGUR EN AS IULUNMOD. AUOV UAD AUON ACNUROP IAS IICINECU ERTAC IULUNMOD ASIZ...
BLESSED BE.

BLESSED BE!
HAIL DRACULA!
BLESSED BE!
UMM...HELLO... I'M SORRY. I REALLY HATE PUBLIC SPEAKING... I'M TERRIBLE AT IT...I'M SUPPOSED TO READ THIS SPEECH...
I'M SORRY, ABRAHAM, IT'S A GREAT SPEECH...I JUST...I'M JUST GOING TO SAY WHAT'S ON MY MIND...
I'M SORRY...I'M NOT SUPPOSED TO BE HERE...MY SISTER...BUT... SHE'S GONE...I'M DRACULA NOW...
MARRY ME!
WHEN I BECAME DRACULA, I ABSORBED THE MEMORIES AND EXPERIENCES OF EVERY WOMAN WHO HAS BORNE THIS LEGACY BEFORE ME.
HUNDREDS OF WOMEN HUNDREDS OF LIFETIMES.
IN ALL OF THOSE LIVES, WE HAVE LEARNED ONE INDISPUTABLE TRUTH: HUMANITY IS IRREDEEMABLE.
HUMANITY THREATENS ALL OF CREATION.
THERE ARE TOO MANY OF YOU...DEEP DOWN, YOU KNOW IT...YOU JUST WON'T ADMIT IT...YOU'RE KILLING THE WORLD... BLEEDING IT DRY...
IS THE WAY
MY SISTER LOVED YOU.
I DON'T.
I HATE YOU.
BUT I WILL SAVE YOU.

I LIKE TO READ. I LOVE MOVIES.
AMERICA GREAT AGAIN!
I READ ALL THESE BOOKS...WATCH ALL THESE MOVIES...ABOUT DYSTOPIAN SOCIETIES.
THEY'RE ALL PRETTY MUCH THE SAME.
SAVIOR
CULA
NOT MY DRACULA
THE GREEDY DID SOMETHING STUPID FOR...WELL...GREED.
IT FUCKED THE WORLD. ALL THE PEOPLE ARE SUFFERING UNDER THEIR OPPRESSION.
A HERO RISES UP FROM THE MASSES TO LEAD THE ENLIGHTENED OPPRESSED IN OVERTHROWING THEIR OPPRESSORS WHO STILL LIVE IN THE DARKNESS OF EXCESS, AVARICE AND GLUTTONY.
I FUCKING HATE THOSE STORIES.
YOU'RE SUPPOSED TO SEE IT AS THE TRIUMPH OF THE HUMAN SPIRIT EVEN AGAINST IMPOSSIBLE ODDS.
YOU'RE SUPPOSED TO APPRECIATE THE OPPORTUNITIES FOR THE FORMERLY OPPRESSED TO REMAKE THE WORLD IN A NEWER, KINDER, MORE EQUITABLE FASHION.
THAT'S NOT HOW I SEE IT.
THAT'S NOT WHAT HAPPENS.

YOU SEE, WHETHER IT'S A MOVIE OR A BOOK OR EVEN A VIDEO GAME...
...THE STORY ALWAYS ENDS AT THE EXACT MOMENT THE OPPRESSED TAKE THEIR FIRST STEPS TOWARD BECOMING THE OPPRESSORS.
BITE ME!
FAVORITE
THE OPPRESSORS DIDN'T START OPPRESSING THE MOMENT THEY BURST FROM THE WOMB.
FUCK...MOST OF THEM NEVER EVEN KNOW THEY'RE OPPRESSING ANYONE.
YOU SUCK BLOOD
THEY NEVER INTENDED TO ENSLAVE THE WORLD.
THEY JUST LIVE THEIR LIVES THE BEST WAY THEY CAN...
...MAKING THE BEST DECISIONS FOR THEM AND FOR THOSE THEY HOLD DEAR.
THEY DIDN'T CHOOSE TO BE THE BAD GUYS.
THEY BECAME THE BAD GUYS BY THE CHOICES THAT THEY MADE.
SEE WHERE I'M GOING WITH THIS?
THOSE PEOPLE LIFTING THOSE OPPRESSIVE BOOTS TO CRAWL OUT FROM THOSE DEPRESSING GUTTERS ARE GOING TO SLIP THOSE SAME BOOTS ON...
...AND MARCH RIGHT INTO THE CATHEDRALS OF OPPRESSION RECENTLY VACATED BY THEIR NOW BAREFOOT PREDECESSORS BLEEDING OUT INTO THE GUTTERS.
THIS IS TH
MARRY ME
THEY'LL LIVE THEIR LIVES AS BEST THEY CAN, MAKING THE BEST DECISIONS FOR THEM AND FOR THE PEOPLE THEY HOLD DEAR.

IN A GENERATION OR TWO OR THREE OR SIX OR TEN THE PLIGHT OF THE NOUVEAU OPPRIMEE WILL ECHO AGAIN FROM THE GUTTERS.
THEY'LL REPEAT THIS CYCLE UNTIL THE SUN DEVOURS THE WORLD MAKING THEM ALL IRRELEVANT AGAIN.
I MAKE NO PRETENSIONS ABOUT BEING THE GOOD GUY. I'M NOT MY SISTER.
IF YOU ARE A PRODUCTIVE MEMBER OF SOCIETY, AN APP IS NOW BEING INSTALLED ON YOUR MOBILE DEVICE.
IT GRANTS YOU UNFETTERED ACCESS TO FOOD, SHELTER, MEDICINE, EDUCATION. EVERYTHING YOU NEED TO LIVE A FULFILLING, PEACEFUL LIFE.
IF YOU DO NOT RECEIVE THIS APP, YOU HAVE BEEN IDENTIFIED AS A BURDEN TO SOCIETY.
YOU WILL BE REMANDED TO THE NEAREST PROCESSING FACILITY.
THERE YOU WILL BE ASSESSED FOR ANY POTENTIAL VALUE YOU MIGHT HAVE.
I DON'T CARE WHO LIVES OR WHO DIES.
I'M EQUALLY DEAF TO THOSE WHO SUFFER AND THOSE WHO THRIVE.
I WANT THEM ALL TO BURN BECAUSE I'M BORED WALKING AROUND IN CIRCLES.
BLESSED BE.

BLESSED BE!
HAIL DRACULA!
BLESSED BE!
HAIL DRACULA!

HAIL DRACULA!
BLESSED BE!
HAIL DRACULA!
BLESSED BE!

IN AMERICA ONE OUT OF EVERY SEVEN CHILDREN LIVES WITH FOOD INSECURITY. THIRTEEN MILLION CHILDREN. STARVING.
THAT'S A DISGRACE. IT IS PROOF THAT HUMANITY IS NOT FIT TO BE FREE.
IF THE WEALTHIEST AND MOST PROSPEROUS NATION THE WORLD HAS EVER KNOWN CANNOT FEED ITS OWN CHILDREN...
...HOW CAN LESS PRIVILEGED NATIONS BE EXPECTED TO DO SO? THEY CAN'T.
DRACULA BRINGS HOPE TO A HOPELESS WORLD.
NO PERSON UNDER DRACULA'S PROTECTION WILL SUFFER NEEDLESSLY FROM TREATABLE DISEASE.
THE THINGS WE HAVE ACHIEVED HERE IN DC WILL FLOURISH AROUND THE WORLD.
WE WILL LEAVE NO CHILD BEHIND.
WE WILL ELIMINATE FOOD INSECURITY AND HOUSING INSTABILITY.
OUR ANTI-POVERTY INITIATIVES ARE THE CORNERSTONES OF OUR FAITH.
THEY ARE WHY HUNDREDS OF THOUSANDS OF GOOD, HONEST, SALT OF THE EARTH PEOPLE HAVE JOINED OUR MOVEMENT.
THE PEOPLE TRUST DRACULA BECAUSE THEY KNOW SHE WILL DO THE THINGS THEY CANNOT BRING THEMSELVES TO DO.
EVEN IF THEY KNOW THEY'RE RIGHT.
QUESTIONS?

MINISTER!
HOW DO YOU ANSWER CLAIMS THAT DRACULA'S ACTIONS ARE ILLEGAL IN A DEMOCRACY? DON'T HER INITIATIVES VIOLATE HUMAN RIGHTS AND LIBERTIES?
THIS IS NO LONGER A DEMOCRACY. IF IT EVER WAS.
A NATION CANNOT CLAIM TO REPRESENT THE WILL OF THE PEOPLE WHEN HALF OF ITS POPULATION IS DENIED THE RIGHT TO PARTICIPATE AND ANOTHER SEGMENT IS TREATED AS THREE-FIFTHS OF A PERSON.
ONE OF DRACULA'S FIRST ACTIONS WAS TO SUSPEND THE BILL OF RIGHTS. LAWS SHOULD PROTECT THE PEOPLE. THEY SHOULDN'T PREVENT DRACULA FROM GIVING THEM WHAT THEY NEED.
YOU SAY THAT DRACULA WILL LEAVE NO ONE BEHIND. THAT DOESN'T SEEM TO GEL WITH HER CONCENTRATION CAMPS.
EVERYONE TAKEN TO OUR PROCESSING CENTERS IS THOROUGHLY EVALUATED AND GIVEN EVERY OPPORTUNITY TO BE A BENEFIT TO SOCIETY. OUR DOCTORS TREAT THEIR AILMENTS.
WE PROVIDE WORLD CLASS EDUCATION AND JOB TRAINING. WE GIVE THEM EVERY TOOL NECESSARY TO BE PRODUCTIVE MEMBERS OF SOCIETY. EVERYONE MUST CONTRIBUTE IN SOME WAY.
YOU SAY THAT EVERYONE MUST CONTRIBUTE IN SOME WAY.
WHAT HAPPENS TO THOSE WHO CAN'T?
HUMANS EXPEND FAR TOO MUCH TIME AND RESOURCES CATERING TO THE NEEDS OF THE EXTREME.
THE EXTREMELY WEALTHY GET ALL OF THE ECONOMIC BREAKS.
THE EXTREMELY POOR SUCK UP ALL THE SOCIAL RESOURCES.
DRACULA'S FOCUS IS ON THE VAST MAJORITY OF THE PEOPLE WHO LAND SOMEWHERE IN BETWEEN.
YES, THAT DOES MEAN THAT THE WORLD WILL MOVE ON WITHOUT SOME PEOPLE. THERE WILL BE FAR FEWER THAN WERE IGNORED BY THE PREVIOUS REGIME.
THANK YOU ALL. NO FURTHER QUESTIONS.

A BIT EARLY ISN'T IT?
LATE. EARLY. I HAVE NO ***FUCKING*** IDEA, ELIZABETH.
I'VE BEEN IN THIS CAVE FOR MONTHS.
WHAT'S WRONG?
I CAN'T CRACK THEIR GENOME. THEY'RE HUMAN, BUT THEY'RE NOT.
THEY REPRODUCE BY PASSING THEIR GENETIC INFORMATION THROUGH DNA IN THE SALIVA. THEY ESSENTIALLY CLONE THEMSELVES WHEN THEY BITE.
THE DNA LIES DORMANT...SOMETIMES FOR YEARS, DECADES EVEN...THEN ONE DAY IT JUST MAGICALLY ACTIVATES. I HAVE NO IDEA HOW OR WHY.
YOU'LL FIGURE IT OUT.
I HOPE SO.
THEY'LL KILL YOU IF YOU DON'T.
I KNOW.

VROOOOM
KRUNK

LOOK AT THEM, EDWARD.
HOW DO THEY LEAD SUCH DISGUSTING LIVES?
POVERTY, MA'AM.
BULLSHIT.
MA'AM?
I WAS POOR ONCE, BUT I WAS NEVER FILTHY.
THEY COULD DO BETTER IF THEY CHOSE. POVERTY IS THEIR EXCUSE NOT TO.
PERPETUAL VICTIMS ETERNALLY BLAMING EVERYONE ELSE FOR THEIR PLIGHT.
I HATE THEM.
THE POOR?
HUMANS.
"BURN IT ALL. LEAVE NO ONE ALIVE."

...
ARE YOU SURE?
GURK
NEVER QUESTION MY ORDERS.
AS YOU SAY, SO IT SHALL BE.

THEY WILL NEVER LOVE YOU.
MAKE THEM FEAR YOU!
INFLICT YOUR WILL WITH SEVERITY.
HIT THEM SO HARD THEY'LL NEVER ENTERTAIN REVENGE.
AS THE BLACK PLAGUE OPENED THE WAY FOR THEIR GOLDEN AGE...
SO WILL YOUR SACRIFICE MAKE WAY FOR A NEW RENAISSANCE.
THEY WILL HATE YOU NOW. THEIR GRANDCHILDREN WILL WORSHIP YOU.
DRACULINA.

AAAIEEEEEEE
PLUCK
DRACU-LA.
SHE'S DRACULINA NO MORE.
APOLOGIES, CARMILLA. DRACULA.
IT'S FINE.
NO. IT IS NOT "FINE."
DECORUM MUST ALWAYS BE OBSERVED.

YOU ARE DRACULA NOW.
YOUR WILL IS SACROSANCT. YOUR WORD IS LAW.
DO AS YOU WILL.
THEIR LIVES ARE YOURS.
YOU ARE BEYOND REPROACH.

ARE YOU READY?
NO.
BUT I'LL DO IT...FOR THEM.
WHAT YOU DO NOW MUST BE DONE.
...
THEY MUST JOIN US. LOVE US OR ELSE HATE US THROUGH DEATH AND AFTER.
THE RESULT IS THE SAME. THERE IS NO OTHER WAY.
BE MERCIFUL. GIVE THEM NO QUARTER.
THESE FEW MUST DIE SO THAT MANY MORE MIGHT LIVE.

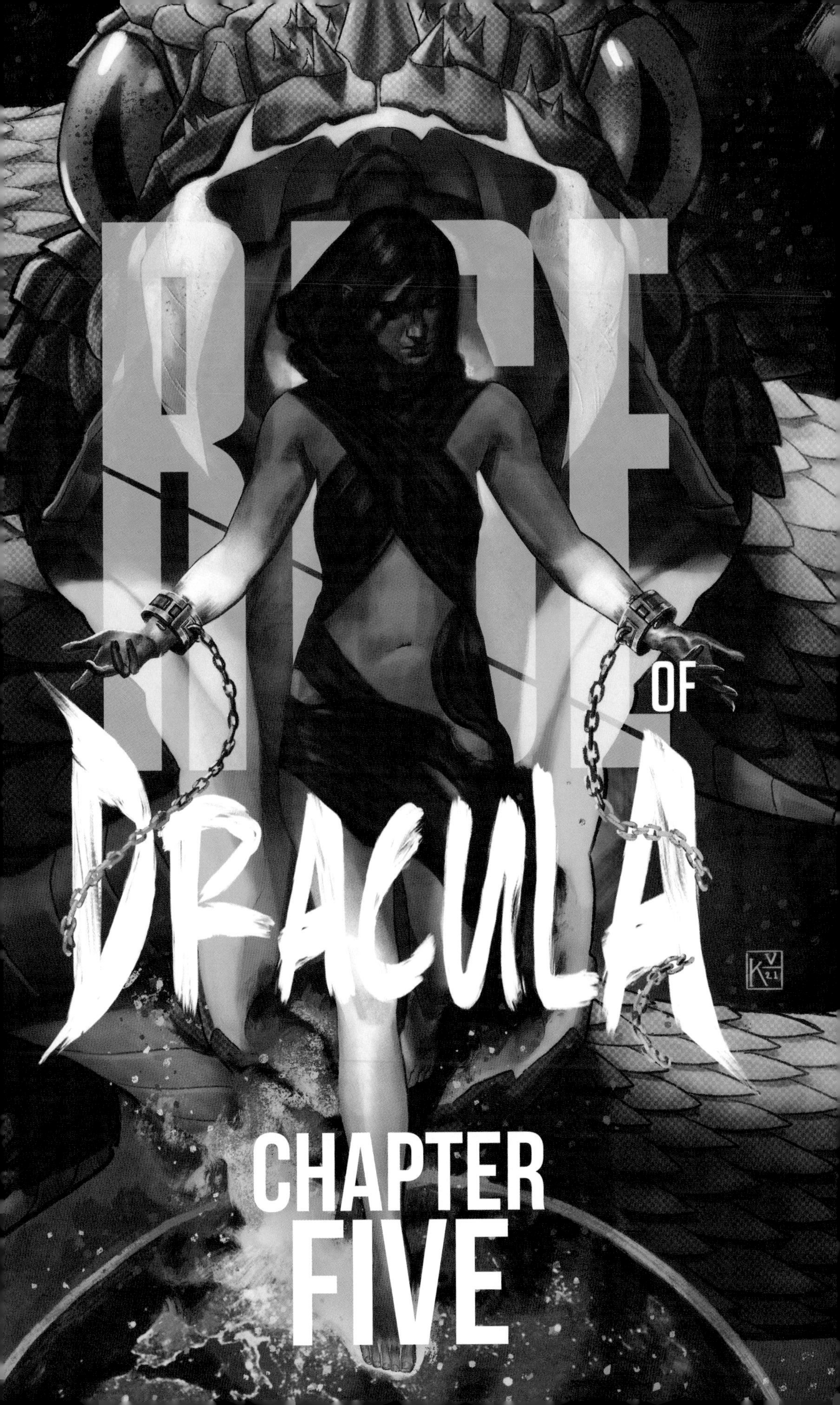
OF
DRACULA
CHAPTER
FIVE

RAGE
OF
DRACULA

Woodland Park Re-Education Center
LIBERTY
RESPONSIBILITY
THE RESPONSIBILITY OF PROSPERITY
AN OFFICIAL RE-EDUCATION DIRECTIVE
SANCTIONED BY THE ORDO DRACUL
♫ OUR EYES HAVE SEEN THE GLORY OF OUR SAVIOR DRACULA. SHE IS ROOTING OUT CORRUPTION AND WILL SEE OUR WORLD RESTORED. ♫
SHE WILL GUIDE US TO THE FUTURE ♫ WITH ENSURED PROSPERITY. HER TRUTH IS MARCHING ON! ♫
PROSPERITY MEANS MANY THINGS TO MANY PEOPLE.

TO A YOUNG GO-GETTER LIKE TREYVON, IT MEANS A WORLD CLASS EDUCATION.
TO AN ENTREPRENEUR LIKE SUSAN, IT MEANS A STABLE ECONOMIC SYSTEM.
FOR A CONCERNED CITIZEN LIKE WILLIAM IT'S A COMFORTABLE RETIREMENT.
WHATEVER PROSPERITY MEANS TO YOU, NEVER FORGET THAT ACHIEVING IT REQUIRES EFFORT FROM US ALL!

THE ORDER GUARANTEES THE STABILITY, SECURITY AND SUSTAINABILITY TO ALL CITIZENS CONTRIBUTING TO OUR NEW GREAT SOCIETY.
THESE PROMISES ARE GIVEN FREELY, BUT THEY ARE NOT GIVEN WITHOUT COST.
GREAT ACHIEVEMENTS REQUIRE GREAT COMMITMENT.
EVERY GOOD CITIZEN MUST REMAIN STEADFAST AGAINST THE CORRUPTIVE INFLUENCE OF DEVIANTS AND DEFECTIVES.
TALK TO YOUR PARENTS. TALK TO YOUR TEACHERS.
THEY'LL SHOW YOU HOW TO SPOT A DEFECTIVE OR A DEVIANT!
GLORY! GLORY! PEACE IN DRACULA!
BY HER GRACE WE WILL PROSPER!
GLORY! GLORY! TO THE ORDER!
OUR WILL IS MARCHING ON!

WHAT IS A DEVIANT? WHAT MAKES A PERSON DEFECTIVE?
CAN YOU THINK OF AN EXAMPLE?
A DUM-DUM?
THAT'S RIGHT, DIEGO! DUM-DUMS MAKE IT HARDER FOR TREYVON TO ACHIEVE HIS FULL ACADEMIC POTENTIAL.
EVERYONE CAN ACHIEVE MORE WITHOUT THE DISTRACTIONS OF DUM-DUMS WHO CAN'T KEEP UP! DUM-DUMS DRAG US ALL DOWN BECAUSE THEY CAN'T.
EVERY MINUTE THAT A TEACHER IS DISTRACTED BY A DUM-DUM IS A MOMENT STOLEN FROM EACH OF YOU. THAT'S NOT FAIR, IS IT?
NOOOOOOO!
BUT WHAT IF IT'S NOT THEIR FAULT? WHAT IF THEY DON'T MEAN TO BE A DUM-DUM?
WHAT IF THEY HAVE A DISABILITY THAT MAKES THEM DUMB?
THAT'S A GREAT QUESTION, RIKKU!
CLASS? DOES ANYONE KNOW THE ANSWER TO RIKKU'S QUESTION?

ANY PERSON WHO CANNOT CONTRIBUTE BECAUSE OF A DISABILITY IS DEFECTIVE.
A GOOD CITIZEN WILL FIND A TRUSTED ADULT OR OFFICER OF THE ORDER TO REPORT THEM IMMEDIATELY.
THE DEFECTIVE WILL THEN BE REMANDED TO THE ORDER FOR PROCESSING.

PERFECTLY STATED, ***JOHNNY!*** I'D BETTER ***WATCH OUT!***
YOU MIGHT BE COMING FOR MY JOB ONE DAY!
HA HA
HA HA HA HA HA HA HA HA HA HA HA HA

WHAT ARE SOME OTHER EXAMPLES OF DEFECTIVES OR DEVIANTS?

CRIMINALS AND THUGS!
PEOPLE WHO REFUSE TO WORK!
PEOPLE WHO DON'T SUPPORT THE ORDER!
ANTI-VAXXERS!
WE'VE ALREADY COVERED DUM-DUMS, PIPER.

MINISTER VAN HELSING?
YES, BRIANNA?
WHAT DOES PROCESSING MEAN?
THANK YOU FOR ASKING SUCH A WONDERFUL QUESTION!
YOU'RE WELCOME!
WELL...
PROCESSING GIVES DEVIANTS AND DEFECTIVES EVERY OPPORTUNITY TO PROVE THAT THEY CAN BECOME CONTRIBUTING CITIZENS OF THE ORDER.
...WHAT HAPPENS IF THEY CAN'T BE CONTRIBUTORS?
THEY'RE SENT TO THE FARMS.
WHAT DO THEY DO THERE?
LET'S SAY THAT THERE IS ONE WAY THAT EVERYONE CAN CONTRIBUTE AND LEAVE IT THERE SHALL WE?

UUURRRRMMMKK
-SIGH-
ISAIAH? WHAT'S ON YOUR MIND SON?
NOTHIN' MAMA.
NO NEED TO BE PROUD AROUND ME, CHILD! I RAISED YOU. I WIPED YOUR TEARS **AND** YOUR ASS.
NOTHIN' LEFT TO HIDE FROM ME. MAMA'S SEEN IT **ALL.**
THINKING ABOUT SNEAKING OFF. TAKING MOLLY. MAKING A NEW START OUT WEST.

FREE STATES?
MMMMHMMM.
THINKING ABOUT JOINING THE RESISTANCE?
NAW! MINA WAS GOOD TO US WHEN SHE WAS DRACULA. WOULDN'T BE RIGHT TO STAB HER IN THE BACK NOW.
EVEN IF SHE IS DEAD.
HEARD YOU SAY YOU'RE TAKING MOLLY WITH YOU. DIDN'T HEAR YOU MENTION AYA'S NAME.
SHE AIN'T GONNA GO.
SHE AIN'T GONNA LET YOU GO. NOT WITH HER CHILD.
THAT'S WHY I SAID I WAS SNEAKING OFF. I DON'T PLAN ON GIVING HER A VOICE ON THE MATTER.
SHE'S YOUR WIFE, ISAIAH. HER VOICE ISN'T YOURS TO GIVE.
YOU'VE MADE A GOOD LIFE HERE, SON. WORK'S UNPLEASANT BUT YOU DO WHAT YOU'VE GOTTA DO FOR YOUR FAMILY.
YOU PUT A ROOF OVER THEIR HEAD AND FOOD IN THEIR BELLY.
A LOT OF FATHERS PROVIDE A LOT LESS.
YOU'RE A GOOD MAN, ISAIAH, EVEN IF YOU'VE GOTTA DO SOME BAD THINGS.

YOU THINK LONG AND HARD BEFORE YOU GO RUNNING OFF AFTER SOMETHING THAT MIGHT NOT BE THERE.
I WILL.
PROMISE?
I PROMISE.
PROMISE.
I SAID I PROMISE, MAMA.
THAT'S THREE TIMES YOU PROMISED. THAT'S A SACRED VOW.
SCHIK
I'D NEVER LIE TO YOU. NOT TO DELTHEA THE HOODOO PRIESTESS. DAMNED SURE NOT TO MY MAMA!
I LOVE YOU, ISAIAH.
I LOVE YOU TOO, MAMA.
YOU GOT WORK TO DO, SON. BEST GET TO DOIN IT.
RECKON I SHOULD.
WALK WITH ME A BIT?
ALWAYS.

HAHAHAHHA
HAHAHAHHA
WOOSH
RUN!!
BLAM
BLAM BLAM
AAA
NO NEED TO RUN! THERE'S PLENTY FOR EVERYONE!
NO NO NO NO NO NO...
GAH!!

AAAAGH!
RRRIIIP
HA HAHA
HAHA HAHA HAHA
HAHA HA
SMASH
AHHHH!

WE'RE WELL UNDER WAY AND SHE'S FAR EXCEEDING OUR EXPECTATIONS. SHE'S NOT EVEN BOTHERING TO SORT THE WHEAT FROM THE CHAFF.
YOU'LL HAVE YOUR MONSTER BY MORNING, LADY RUTHVEN.
SHE'S MAD, CARMILLA.
SHE'S ALREADY A MONSTER. WE NEED ONLY SHOW THAT TO THE WORLD.
I BELIEVE THAT'S MY DEPARTMENT.
IT'S ALL BEEN ARRANGED. THE 'NERO NARRATIVE' IS SET TO GO LIVE ON ALL SOCIAL MEDIA OUTLETS BY YOUR COMMAND, LADY RUTHVEN.
ONCE UPON A TIME, ONE NEEDED AN ARMY TO SACK A CITY.
NOW ONE PERSON CAN TOPPLE AN EMPIRE FROM THE PALM OF HER HAND.
ARMIES STILL HAVE THEIR PLACE IN REVOLUTIONS. OURS WILL BE READY WHEN THE TIME COMES.

WELL, FUCK ME.
IT ISN'T DNA.
VICTOR?
IT'S A VIRUS.
IT'S A BLOODY, **FUCKING** VIRUS.
HA HA HA
I JUST KNEW YOU'D CRACK IT.
I **NEVER** LOST FAITH IN YOU.

APOLOGIES. SCIENCE IS SLOW. WE NEED MORE TIME.
TIME IS SUDDENLY IN SHORT SUPPLY.
AL-DAJJAL IS SURPRISINGLY COMPETENT AT GENOCIDE.
I HAVE IT!
AND WHAT IS IT YOU HAVE, BROTHER FRANKENSTEIN?
DOOT
DOCTOR FRANKENSTEIN.
AFTER THIS, YOU'D BLOODY WELL BETTER REMEMBER IT.

HUWAKK
I'M DYING.
YOU'RE NOT DYING.
YOU'RE JUST PURGING ALL THAT PURE, CONCENTRATED EVIL.
I ONLY HAD ONE WHITE CLAW.
IT WAS PUMPKIN SPICE, WASN'T IT?
YES...
WE WERE JUST IN TIME.
ANY LATER AND OUR BELOVED SISTER WOULD BE...GONE.
LOST TO THE REALM OF BASIC WHITE BITCHES FOREVER.
WANDERING ETERNITY IN UGGS, LEGGINGS A PUFFER VEST AND THAT GODAWFUL MESSY PONYTAIL!
I DUNNO. I THINK SHE'D LOOK CUTE WITH A MESSY PONYTAIL.
IS THERE ANYTHING YOU DON'T LOOK GOOD IN?
THE TOILET?
NOPE! HEAD HUNG IN THE TOILET IN A ROLLER DISCO STRIP CLUB IN HELL...
...VOMIT RUNNING DOWN YOUR CHIN, FACE WET FROM PISS WATER AND I'LL BET YOU CAN STILL CATCH A DICK!
YEAH, BUT GUYS ARE EASY.
I COULD CATCH A DICK TONIGHT IF I WANTED...AND I DON'T EVEN HAVE A BODY.
GOT DEM LIPS THO.
WUB WUB WUB

GUYS... DO YOU THINK...DO YOU THINK THIS IS REALLY IT? LIKE, THIS IS WHERE OUR STORY ENDS.
NO PURPOSE.
NO ACCOMPLISHMENTS.
NO RELATIONSHIPS. JUST THREE HOT AS FUCK BITCHES PARTYING IN HELL UNTIL...UM... WHAT HAPPENS AFTER HELL?
SUPER HELL?
IS THAT A SIMPSONS REFERENCE?
FAMILY GUY.
WHICH MEANS IT WAS PROBABLY A SIMPSONS REFERENCE FIRST.
THIS CAN'T BE ALL THERE IS...RIGHT?
LIKE, WHY WOULD "GOD"...WHO ACTUALLY EXISTS AND I'M TOTALLY SHOCKED BY THAT KNOWLEDGE BY THE WAY...
RIGHT?
IF HE'S, YOU KNOW, GOD...WHY WOULD HE CREATE US THEN NEVER DO ANYTHING WITH US?
ALL I'VE EVER DONE... MY ENTIRE LIFE...
...ALL I'VE EVER DONE IS EAT, DRINK, FUCK AND TAKE A TRULY LUDICROUS AMOUNT OF DRUGS.

SURELY THAT'S NOT IT, RIGHT? THERE'S MORE? I DON'T WANT TO BE FORGOTTEN LIKE THIS.
AWWW! HONEY! OF COURSE THERE'S MORE. JUST BECAUSE YOU HAVEN'T DONE ANYTHING YET DOESN'T MEAN YOU WON'T.
I'D HUG YOU RIGHT NOW ELLIE, BUT...I WELL...NO HANDS.
WANNA GO DOWN TO CHARON'S MARINA?
TORMENT THE NEW ARRIVALS?
UH HUH.
WANNA PRETEND WE'LL MAKE OUT WITH THEM BUT THEN LOCK THEM IN THAT CREEPY ROOM AT THE END OF THE HALL WHERE I SAW THAT THREE HEADED DOG THING?
HELL YEAH!

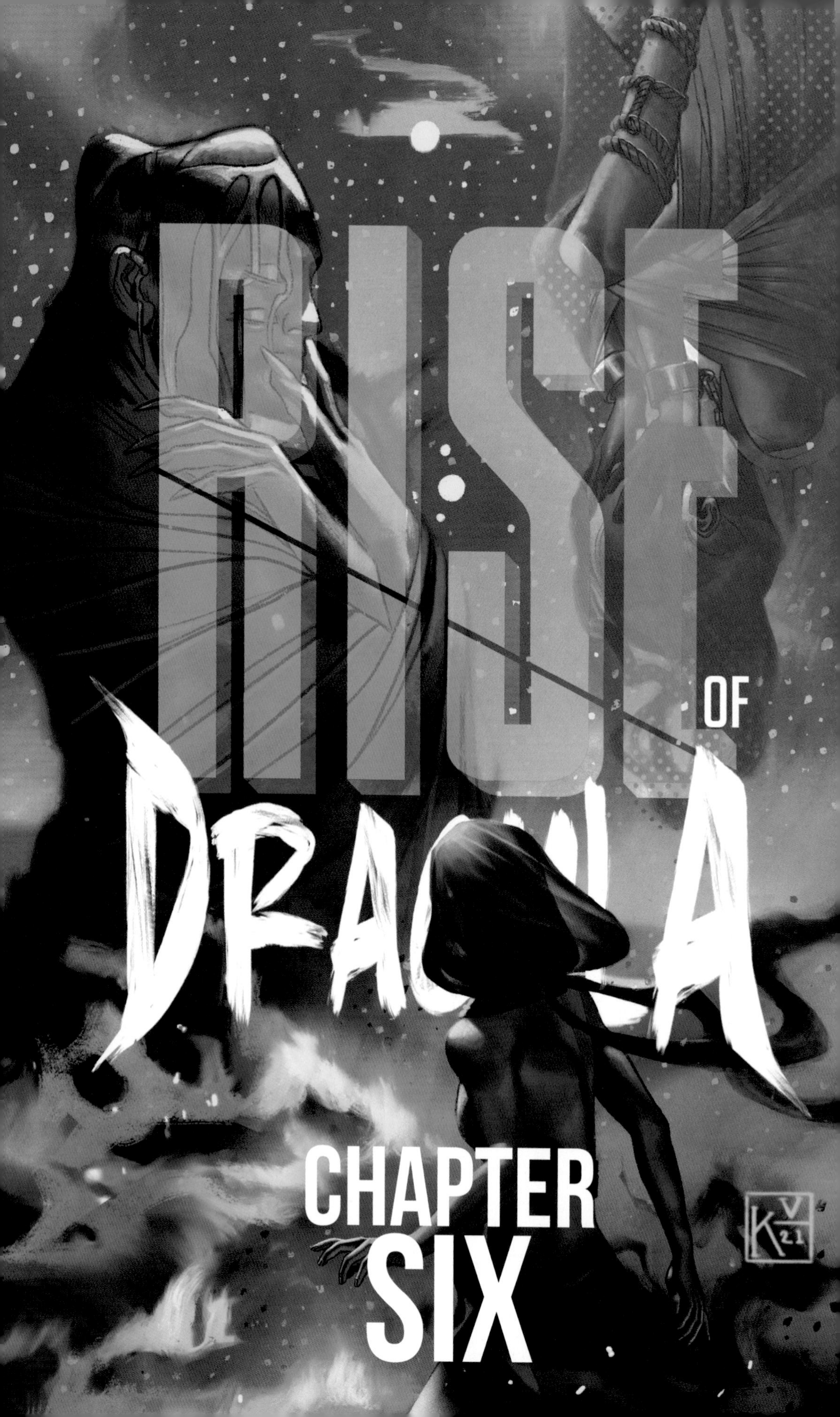
RISE
OF
DRACULA
CHAPTER
SIX

"BEHOLD, THE PEOPLE RISE LIKE A LIONESS; THEY ROUSE THEMSELVES LIKE A LION, NOT RESTING UNTIL THEY DEVOUR THEIR PREY AND DRINK THE BLOOD OF THE SLAIN."

NUMBERS 23:24

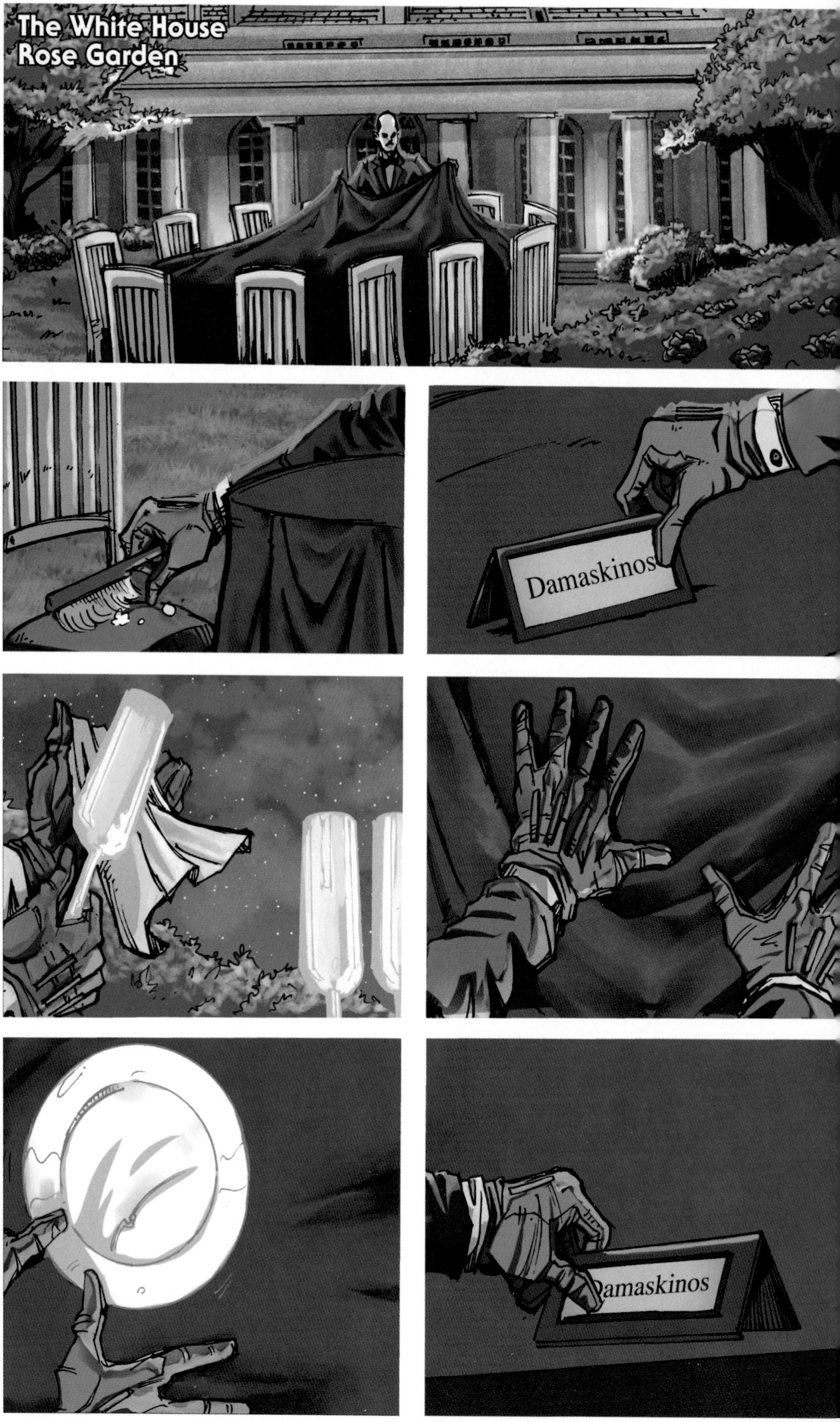
The White House
Rose Garden
Damaskinos
Damaskinos

Orlock
Manrugo
Ruthven

WELL HELLO, YOUNG MAN.
HELLO.
MIND IF I SIT A SPELL?
NO.
MY NAME IS DELTHEA. MAY I ASK YOURS?
ROONE.
ISN'T THAT AN INTERESTING NAME.
I GUESS SO.
WHAT ARE YOU DOING IN HERE ALL ALONE, MR. ROONE?
I'M NOT SURE. SOME MEN CAME TO MY HOUSE AND TOOK ME TO A FARM. I SAW COWS AND CHICKENS AND DUCKS.
THEY LET ME PET THE DOG. HIS NAME WAS TAZ BECAUSE HE'S SO CRAZY.
THEN SOME OTHER MEN CAME AND BROUGHT ME HERE. THEY SAID I COULD BE USEFUL.
I WANTED TO HELP. MAMA SAYS IT'S ALWAYS GOOD TO BE HELPFUL. HELPFUL MEANS ALMOST THE SAME AS USEFUL. MAYBE IF I'M A HELPER, I CAN GO HOME AND MAMA WON'T CRY ANYMORE.
SHE WAS SAD WHEN THE MEN TOOK ME AWAY.
I DIDN'T MEAN TO MAKE MAMA CRY.

OH SWEET CHILD. LITTLE BOYS ALWAYS MAKE MOTHERS CRY, BUT IT'S NOT YOUR FAULT.
SHE JUST LOVES YOU SO MUCH SHE CAN'T HOLD IT IN.
NOW YOU LISTEN TO GRANNY DELTHEA, YOU HEAR?
YOUR MAMA LOVES YOU. YOU'RE A GOOD BOY.
A BRAVE BOY. YOUR MAMA IS PROUD OF YOU.
YOU **WILL** SEE HER AGAIN.
BYE, GRANNY DELTHEA. I'M GONNA GO BE A HELPER NOW!
GOODBYE, ROONE. DON'T FORGET WHAT I SAID.
YOU ARE A GOOD BOY. YOU ARE LOVED.

RIGHT THIS WAY, LADY RUTHVEN.

JESUS!
CLANG
BZZKKZT
ROOAARR
BZZKKZT
BZZKKZT
ARGGH!
SPLUT

George Washington Memorial Pkwy
WE'RE APPROACHING A LARGE NUMBER OF PROTESTORS, LADY RUTHVEN.
WE'LL NEED TO STOP.
NO.
VRRRMM
RUN!!
BY YOUR COMMAND.
UNGH
AAAIEEE
SPLUT
BLARGH

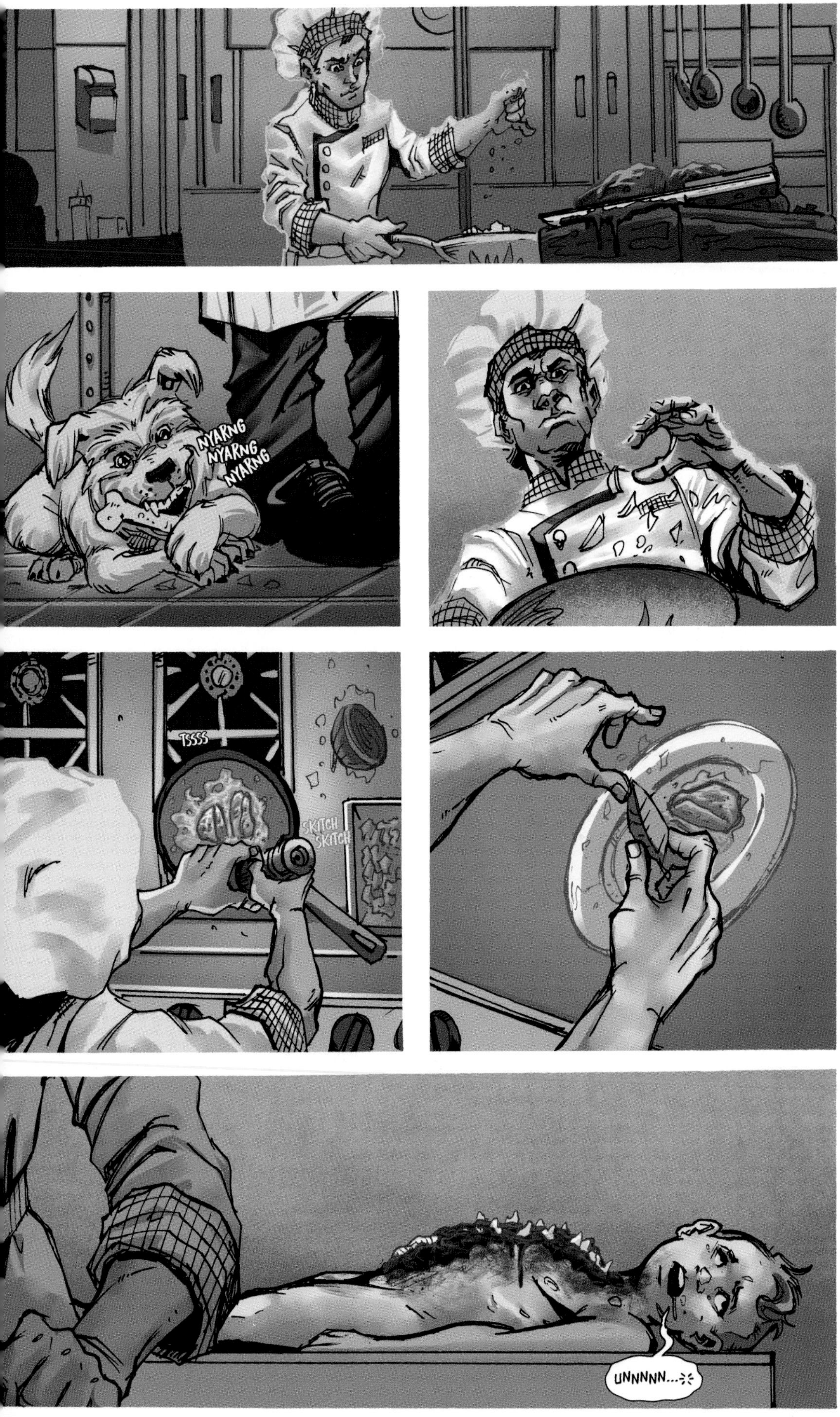
NYARNG
NYARNG
NYARNG
TSSSS
SKITCH
SKITCH
UNNNNN...

Lily FOR MAYOR '24!
GEN 1:26
WE ARE ALL USEFUL
HI, MOM!
OUR LIVES MATTER
MAYOR '24!
STAND BACK.
WHORE!
DIE!
VAMPIRES
FASCIST!
CHOK
WHAK
FASCIST BITCH!

HOW ABOUT A KISS?
EAT GLASS!
OUR LIVES
GET THEM OFF!
ALL
USEFUL
AAHHHHHHHHH!

WHA--
AAHHHHHH!
GET THEM OFF ME!
OUR LIVES MATTER
GEN 1:26
EAT GLASS!
BLAM
BLAM
BLAM
ARGH!
RUN!!
KRAK
YEAH!!
THUD
VRRRRM

DON'T BE AFRAID.

IT'S ONLY DARKNESS.
MOTHER?
MY UNFORTUNATE DAUGHTER, HOW DISAPPOINTING YOU ARE.
FUCK. YOU. MOTHER!

HAHAHAHAHAH
RRRRRRRMURRRRRRR

I'M NO VULCAN, BUT THE LOGIC HERE IS PRETTY CLEAR.
THE NEEDS OF THE MANY DO INDEED OUTWEIGH THE NEEDS OF THE FEW.
"AREN'T WE THE FEW?"
OH NO, MARK. WE'RE THE ONLY.
"THE ONLY ONES THAT MATTER ANYWAY."
YOU SHOULD COME WORK FOR ME.
"HARD PASS."
I ONLY WORK FOR VAMPIRES I CAN TRUST.

OF COURSE I DON'T FEEL SORRY FOR THEM. THEY'VE NO ONE TO BLAME BUT THEMSELVES.
IF THEY'D SPEND AS MUCH TIME WORKING AS "LIVING THEIR BEST LIVES" THEY MIGHT ACTUALLY HAVE A LIFE WORTH LIVING!
IF THEY CAN AFFORD AN IPHONE, WHY CAN'T THEY PAY RENT?!"
"BUT THEY DON'T WANT TO PAY RENT. THEY THINK THEY'RE OWED A PLACE TO LIVE."
WE ARE NOT DEFECTIVE!
WORSE! THEY EXPECT US TO PAY FOR IT.
AND THEY CALL US CRIMINALS!
MAKE VAMPIRES AFRAID AGAIN!
"IN MY TWO MILLENNIA ON THIS EARTH, HUMANITY HAS PROVEN TWO CONSTANTS: LAZINESS AND FILTH."
PHYSIOLOGY ISN'T ALL THEY SHARE WITH PIGS!
"MUD, TRASH AND FILTH ARE ALL HUMANS LEAVE TO MARK THEIR PASSING."
GRROOOAAARR
"IF THEY'RE GOING TO BEHAVE LIKE ANIMALS, WE'VE NO CHOICE BUT TO TREAT THEM AS SUCH."

GRRARGH
RRIIIP
RRAH!
AAAACK!
GET THEM!
SHICK

WHUP
WHUP
WHUP
BRAKKA
BRAKKA
SPLUT
BRAKKA
BRAKKA
BRAKKA
BRAKKA
SPLUT
SPLUT
SPLUT
GRAHHH!
BRAKKA
BRAKKA
BRAKKA
BRAKKA
SKRAK
KABOOM

SKRAK
HRRUCK
WILL YOU...
CRAK
LOVE...
WHUD
ME...
SLISH
NOW?
THOK
NO.
WHYY!?
LOP

FALLEN! FALLEN! FALLEN!
THE REIGN OF MAN IS ENDED.
NOW BEGINS THE REIGN OF
DRACULA

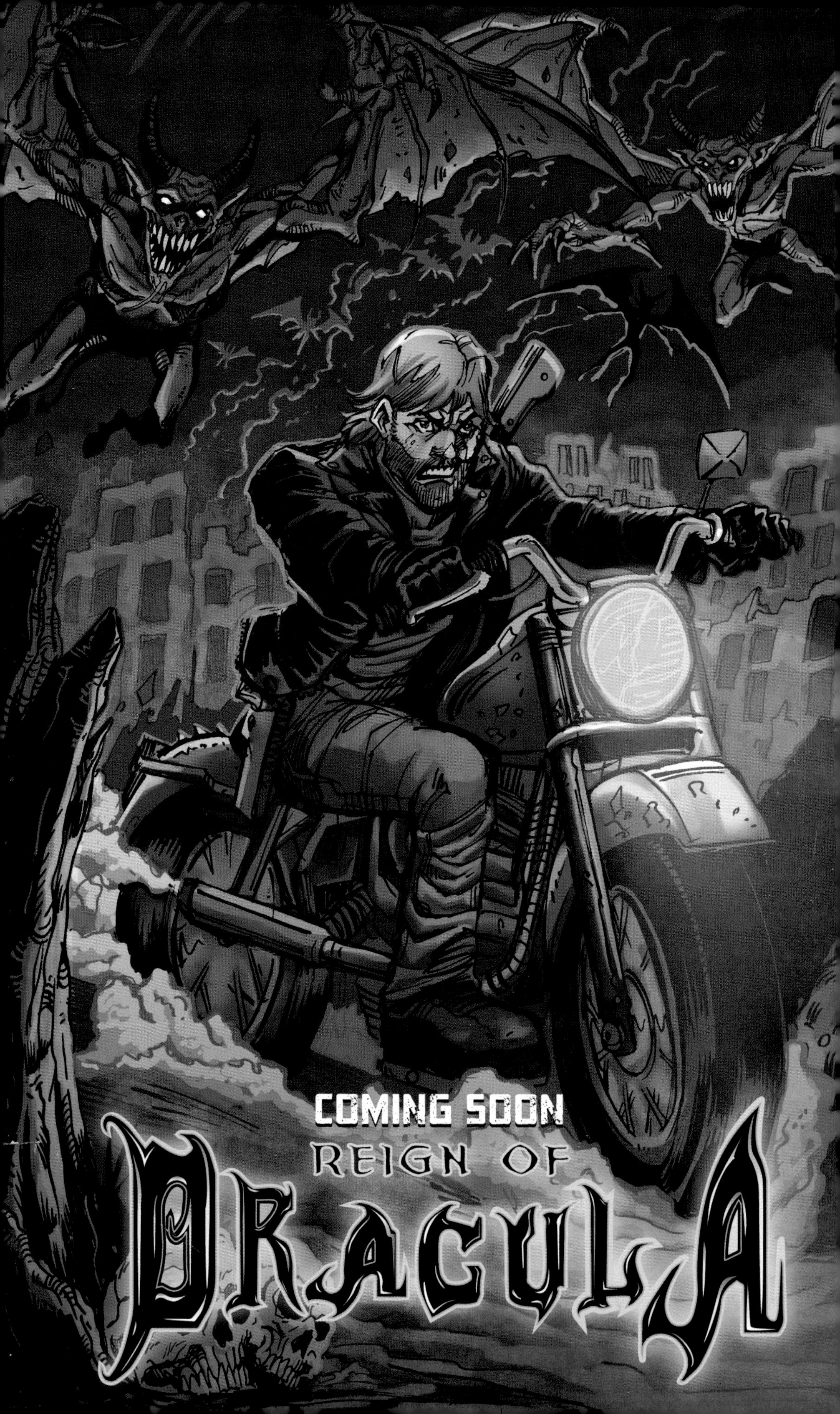
COMING SOON
REIGN OF
DRACULA

GASP